SO-BNZ-565

"I wish I had some asbestos gloves so I could handle fire without getting burned."

Merry's laugh caused my skin to tingle. She touched my arm. "After supper," she promised, "we'll see how much heat you can handle."

As soon as I'd finished eating I sat on our log stool to kick off my thongs. Before the second thong dropped, she was kneeling in front of me. Her eyes held mine as she reached up and began undoing the buttons of my shirt. "This," she said, concentrating on a button, "is how you start a fire."

She opened another button, then another, until my shirt fell open. "Stand up" she whispered, her hands on my hips.

Shakily, I stood.

Slowly she unzipped my jeans and pulled them down around my ankles. "Step out."

She reached up and touched my breasts. I made a move to kneel. "No, stay where you are."

So I stood in the firelight, her hands moving slowly down my naked body.

"Now," she breathed, pulling my hips forward until I could feel the warm puffs of air as she spoke, "now we'll fan the flame. . . .'

To The Lightning

by Catherine Ennis

The Naiad Press Inc.
1988

Copyright © 1988 by Catherine Ennis

All rights reserved. No part of this book may be reproduced or transmitted in any form electronic or mechanical without permission in writing from the publisher.

Printed in the United States of America
First Edition

Edited by Katherine V. Forrest
Cover design by The Women's Graphic Center
Typesetting by Sandi Stancil

Library of Congress Cataloging-in-Publication Data

Ennis, Catherine, 1937 —
    To the lightning / by Catherine Ennis.
        p.   cm.
    ISBN 0-941483-06-1 : $8.95
        I. Title.
    PS3555.N6T6 1988
    813'.54--dc 19   87-31183
                                                                        CIP

About the Author

Originally from Georgia, Catherine Ennis still lives in the deep south, commenting that she "never did like cold weather." Recently retired from teaching, she lives with her lover of fifteen years, three dogs and four cats, spending her free time gardening and trying out a lifetime of unused gourmet recipes. *To The Lightning* is her first novel. There will be many others.

*To Johanna
on her birthday with love.*

Chapter I

Sylvia's lesbian love affairs, which she sandwiched between three marriages, were the choice topics of conversation in all the smart places. But an invitation to one of her parties didn't necessarily mean you were gay. The guest list was as varied as Sylvia's moods. Some of her parties were mixed, some straight, some exclusively gay or whatever combination Sylvia thought would be interesting.

And then there was me. I didn't fit into any particular category except that of Sylvia's friend.

We had been college roommates and had remained close over the years. In our freshman year Sylvia discovered the joys of lesbian sex. Not with me. I was too shy and uncomfortable about sex to have it with anyone, even if I had been asked.

I can't remember how many hours I spent in the library so that Sylvia could swoon in the arms of her newest lover in the privacy of the dorm room she and I shared. "Be a love, will you?" And she'd hold my chin in her hand and look at me with her luminous eyes. At my nod, and I'd always say yes, she'd wink, kiss my cheek and run for the phone. Sometimes I'd meet the girl as I left the building. After a year or so, I even had the courage to nod hello to Sylvia's newest flame as we passed on the steps of the hall.

It was my ambition to work with my father as a tax attorney. So I did the very best I could, studied hard, wrote my papers and went to all my classes. My mother had died when I was two and Father had devotedly taken over my care. It hadn't been easy for him to build a successful business and raise a demanding little girl, but he'd managed to do both. Throughout my childhood I could always count on his love and gentle patience. Both my father and I were looking forward to the day I could move into the office next to his. I learned all I could so that he would feel proud of me. This single-minded purpose didn't leave me time for socializing but I was in school to learn, not to play.

Sylvia, bright and quick with that steel trap mind of hers, seldom went to classes. The fact that the interest from her trust alone could have bought a large slice of the eastern seaboard may have contributed to her lack of interest in academic matters.

We were like night and day. She, tiny with radiant blonde hair, soft curves and huge green eyes; me, tall with hair as straight and black as an Indian's, no figure to speak of and eyes of nothing brown. It may have been our differences that made us friends but friends we had remained.

My father died suddenly, right after graduation. I inherited the business. Once the shock of his death had worn off I moved into his large office and turned the smaller one that was to have been mine into a private waiting room for my clients. I vowed to continue what my father had worked so hard to accomplish.

In the ten years since, I had taken in two partners, computerized the entire operation, hired a dozen more people for the accounting section, and in spite of a competent staff, stayed busy well into the evening and over most weekends.

My shyness prevented me from making friends easily. Sylvia said I had always appeared too uppity and people thought I was judging them, to their disadvantage. "You're too cold, darling, and much too abrupt. You turn people off when you don't smile. Try acting friendly, won't you?"

I had tried but I wasn't a good actress, either, so I retreated behind my desk, made a lot of money, had only two friends, one cat, and a dream of soft hands touching me.

Weekends had meant long hours stretching before me and no way of shortening their slow passing. I did buy groceries but ate most meals out. My cat, who barely put up with me, ate at home and hissed when I picked her up.

There were people who did things for me. The doorman saw that strangers would not approach me; the cleaning lady took care that my apartment was spotless; my clothes were cleaned and pressed by someone; the paper boy put papers in my box; mechanics kept my car running; the lot attendant parked my car and fetched it for me; bankers banked my money and dentists kept my teeth white.

I had contact with the people in my office, joined in the office parties, contributed gifts for showers and remembered birthdays. But at five o'clock they left for a home and a family and I went to my apartment and the cat.

This was simply the way I lived. I did not feel sorry for myself. I was living the life I had made. If I wanted it to be different, I could make changes. The fact that I didn't was proof that I must be satisfied. At least so I told Sylvia.

I was three pages into the twenty pages of some new tax laws I needed to study when Sylvia called. I knew it was Sylvia before I answered. Only she would call in on the private line reserved for my outgoing calls. So I answered, "Hello, Sylvia."

"Oh, darling, you knew it was me. Our ESP is still working, isn't it?"

One eye still on the crowded page, I nodded. "Guess so, dear, what do you need?"

She made a tsk, tsk sound. "Are you too busy to talk to me? I have something very important to tell you."

Sighing, I asked, "Who is she?"

"She? What makes you think it's a she?" Her laugh was teasing. "But you're right, it is a she; only it's a she for you, darling."

"For me? What are you talking about, Sylvia? Make sense, will you?"

Every so often Sylvia would find some woman or man and insist that I meet the person. "Perfect for you," she'd say, "I've found the perfect person just for you."

Sylvia lowered her voice. "Chris, this time I'm really serious. I'm having a party tomorrow night and I want you to be here. I won't tell you who it is you're going to meet but I want you here!"

I was intrigued in spite of myself. I was curious to see the kind of person Sylvia had selected this time.

"All right, I'll come to your party."

"Chris, how can you be so calm when tomorrow night is going to change your life?"

"Sylvia," I said, "don't exaggerate."

As it turned out, she wasn't exaggerating at all.

— 4 —

* * * * *

The special person Sylvia introduced me to was Candy Howard, who was new in town. Right away I liked Candy's friendly smile and the casual way she related to people. I also liked her short dark hair and grey eyes. She seemed to like me, too.

She was a teacher and soon had me laughing at the antics of her fourth graders. It was obvious that she enjoyed her work.

We filled plates at the buffet and found a table by the pool. I was comfortable with her as we sipped Sylvia's Dom Perignon and ate delicious hors d'oeuvres. And talked. I astonished myself by asking her to have dinner with me on Sunday and was delighted when she accepted without hesitation. I was happy to think I had made a friend. An attractive friend. Sunday night couldn't come soon enough.

* * * * *

At Victor's Restaurant we were treated like royalty. I can't recall what we ate but it was probably delicious. We toasted each other with champagne and I felt relaxed as we talked and talked.

Her green dress left some of her shoulders bare and was open part way down the front. I could not make my eyes behave. Her breasts were like a magnet, drawing me time after time and she knew where I was looking. Once, when I managed to lift my gaze, I met her amused eyes. She raised her eyebrows and gave me a tiny smile as if to ask did I like what I saw. I felt myself blushing, the blood making my face and neck hot.

I took the long way home, driving as slowly as I could. Neither of us had much to say. I wanted to make clever conversation but without candlelight and soft music, and without food to keep my hands busy, I was at a loss. Thoughts were shimmering on my brain like heat waves but they disappeared into air when my mouth tried to form them into words.

I found a parking place at the front of her building. Candy was sitting half turned towards me and her arm was across the back of the seat. She leaned slightly toward me and touched my cheek with her fingertips. "Will you come up for a nightcap?"

Would I? There was nothing in the world I wanted more.

We had the elevator to ourselves, and again we stood apart and silent. Her perfume, fainter now, seemed to fill my senses. I stood behind her as she put her key in the lock and I had an overpowering urge to touch her. I had to clench my teeth hard to keep my arms by my side.

When we entered the apartment I took only a step or two inside the room, then stood watching as she closed the door and fastened the chain. I was standing so close that when she turned from the door we were almost toe to toe. I wanted so much to have her touch my face again.

She smiled at me and, without missing a breath, stepped into my arms and raised her face and kissed me. It seemed the most natural thing in the world. Our lips fit. Our bodies fit.

I had ached to touch her and now she was pressed to me, her lips moving under mine. We stood there for a long minute and then, helpless to resist the impulse, I moved my mouth to her shoulder and kissed the warm flesh. I was almost dizzy from the flood of sensation that swept through me as her arms tightened.

We finally paused for breath. Candy, her eyes shining, moved away from me and took my hand. We walked down the hall into the bedroom. Not a word passed between us.

I stood silent and shaking in the darkness as Candy slowly removed my clothing, her hands lingering on my breasts. She kissed and touched and kissed them again. I felt her warm breath as her lips moved over my bare skin. My voice was gone, I could only take in quick short breaths, nothing more was possible.

Then it was my turn to undress her. Trembling, clumsy, I slid her dress down past her shoulders, pinning her arms and leaving bare those smooth mounds that had so tantalized me all evening. Now I became bold. I bent and pressed my lips to that soft flesh. She made a sound deep in her throat. Encouraged, I took the nipple into my mouth, touching it with my tongue.

All questions about my sexuality were forever answered as I tasted the sweetness of her breasts. I knew, as my lips circled the rigid softness, that this was how it was meant to be.

"Chris, unzip me," she breathed. I did, and she shrugged out of the rest of her clothing then pressed her body to mine. We stood, naked, and kissed and touched some more. The feel of her pressed to me was delight past all experience.

She moved us to the bed. We lay facing each other, our mouths joined in lingering kisses, our hands moving, touching, stroking. Without asking, I moved so that I was lying on her, every part of me touching her. She opened her legs and wrapped them around mine.

I kissed her mouth, her ears, all of her face, then her mouth again. I pressed my flesh to hers. We were both breathing hard. She was moving her hips under me and her hands were pulling me closer.

"Love me," she whispered, "love me now!"

"I want to . . . I want to! But I don't know how!"

Her movements stopped. In the dim light from the hall she stared up at me. "You don't . . . know . . . *how?*"

It was then that I told her she was the first. "I should have known," she sighed, "Oh, I should have known!"

Then she moved to lie at my side and lowered her lips to mine in a kiss of such deliberate intensity that I felt jolts, an electric current, flashing from my mouth to the wetness between my legs.

She cupped my breast in a hand and took the tip in her mouth. As she touched me with her tongue and teeth I felt her hand moving down my body.

I had read of lovemaking between women. I had even heard Sylvia describe some lover's technique, or lack of it. All of this I was aware of but I could not have imagined the sweet agony as Candy's hand began moving rhythmically, dipping into the moisture, teasing, pressing lightly, then harder, then more...

My insides turned molten. My body was responding without instructions from me. Candy moved down my body, tantalizing with her tongue, her fingers lightly brushing my flesh. She paused to push my legs farther apart then bent her head and I felt the first soft touch of her tongue.

I had my first orgasm that night and my tenth or my hundredth, who was counting?

Candy taught me to make love to her and I thrilled as her body arched beneath mine. I feasted on her, the flame inside me burning higher and higher. Our bodies were moving together in a rhythm that had no beginning and no end.

It came to me once, as her fingers moved inside me, that someone had once said that now was the time to be happy.

Why had I waited so long?

Chapter II

She was in the shower when I awoke. I could hear the water splashing and I believed I also heard her humming. Since I did not know the correct behavior in these circumstances, I stayed in bed although I desperately needed to use the bathroom.

After a few minutes she came naked into the bedroom, completely unselfconscious, toweling her body dry. I couldn't pretend to be asleep because that would mean my eyes had to be closed and I was enjoying the sight of her. She sat on the edge of the bed and I pulled the cover up to my chin.

"Oh, my," she said, shaking her head in amusement.

After what we had done together in the night on the very same bed, it did seem ridiculous to hide myself from her when she certainly had nothing hidden from me. Honesty being the best policy, I managed to blurt, "Candy, I have to go to the bathroom."

"Of course, my love." And she got up from the bed, leaving the way clear for me to wrap myself in the spread or simply stalk naked across the room.

The old me would have wrapped herself like the Pharaoh's mummy but I remembered developing a different philosophy during the night. My new motto was "Be Happy" and my new behavior was going to reflect this. So I threw back the cover, swung my legs over the side of the bed, grabbed Candy by the shoulders and kissed her squarely on the mouth, then ran for the toilet.

I could hear her laughing all the way.

* * * * *

On the way home I became so hungry that I stopped at a diner and ate a huge breakfast. During the meal I considered staying home all day so that I could replay the evening in the privacy of my own home but there were too many appointments to keep. Besides, I asked myself, would the new me stay home? Would staying home make me happy? I decided that I'd be happier in my office.

I called the florist nearest Candy's building and made arrangements for an immediate delivery of flowers with a note that said, *Call me right away* and signed *Chris*.

When my secretary announced Candy I pushed the button with a hand that actually trembled. I tried to make my voice brisk and businesslike but I managed only a weak "Hello."

"Hi, doll." Her voice was close and warm. "How about dinner?"

Now that we had made contact my new self could take over. That happy, confident person that I had become.

"Yes," I answered. "At my place."

I told her where I lived. She said, "See you, Doll," and hung up.

I called a neighborhood restaurant from the office, and ordered enough food for a banquet to be delivered. I hurried home.

She was just as I remembered her. Hardly waiting until my door was closed, we embraced and kissed . . . and kissed.

The new me said, "I've thought about you all day." The new me said, "I've wanted you all day."

Somehow we made our way to the couch, leaving a trail of clothing in our wake.

She made love to me, her breathing rapid and harsh as she carried me to the top of the mountain with her fingers and tongue. For a long moment I hung there, free, at the apex of the world's highest peak. Then the spasms began and I fell, my body shuddering, uncontrolled. I know I cried out. I probably wailed like a banshee. At any rate, when I came to my senses, she was holding me in her arms, tenderly brushing back the hair from my forehead, saying, "Yes, darling. Yes, love, yes . . ."

At that moment, if the room had burst into flame, I could not have crawled to the door.

Eventually the food came and we ate. Eventually we made love in the shower, in the bed and on the living room floor. We also used the couch again. I was insatiable.

Candy said, "Chris, you're insatiable!" I agreed. I had to make up for lost time. Did we sleep at all that night? Who knows? Did we discuss serious things, like should we go away together? Should we stay together? Should we marry or just live together?

Probably. But I don't remember. I do remember the deep satisfaction as we pleasured each other. We may not have invented anything new, but we certainly tried everything old. The night was a thousand hours that passed with the wink of an eye.

* * * * *

I was a changed person. I was not the same dull work horse I had been. I put on weight, although I should have been worn down to bare bones considering all of the nighttime activity in which Candy and I engaged.

Once it had been my studies but now it was my work that I used as a substitute for the personal commitments other people made. Other people had people, I had my work. Before, taking courses at the university had been the way I spent my evenings. I had learned to forage for wild foods . . . although there were not many wild edibles growing in the hallways of the buildings where I spent most of my time. It was a safe feeling, however, to know that I could prepare cattails or dandelion greens if I found them peeping out from under a carpet. I also learned to throw clay, making fairly credible crockery in which to cook the wild foods when I found them. I wove baskets from store-bought reeds, made colorful designs of glass, tuned windchimes, created copper jewelry, smoked meat and made interesting things like vests from my own hand-carded wool. I could even make brooms and brushes.

It had simply been a way of passing time. I realized now that I had been very busy being busy because I had nothing else to do.

Now it was a different story. Candy came to live with me.

Candy was home from her teaching job before me, usually, and the table was set and the apartment smelling of delicious things to eat when I came flying in the door.

I wanted to shower her with diamonds but she wouldn't hear of it. So I substituted a bottle of wine or flowers or tickets to something special she wanted to see, and sometimes funny things that we could both laugh about. And occasionally something a little more expensive because I couldn't help myself.

Our nights were ecstasy. I don't know that we got any sleep at all the first weeks we were together. Not only the nights. How many lovely dinners burned to a crisp because I couldn't wait for night and bed.

The weekends that had been so long for me were now not long enough. When Friday afternoon came, we would throw clothes in a suitcase, leave food for the cat and head out in my car. Usually we had no particular destination in mind. We'd go to the beach, explore antique shops, visit museums, rent a motel and make love.

Neither of us had a family. Candy seldom mentioned people other than the teachers at the school where she taught. It was as if we were the center of a universe and other people revolved around us, not attracting much of our attention but there nevertheless.

I had never felt so fulfilled.

Sylvia said, "Being in love has improved you, darling." To Candy she'd say, "I'm glad Chris has finally found someone to love."

Neither Candy nor I would soon tire of each other, of this I felt sure. If what we shared wasn't love, then it was good enough for the time being.

* * * * *

The phone call came through the office switchboard. A male voice asked for me by name and spoke other words, and when I said, "Yes, the car you describe is mine," I knew what his next words would be.

Candy had borrowed my car and this was the time of day she would be driving home, to the place we shared, driving to our home.

As he continued speaking, his voice officially sorrowful, I put the phone back in its cradle and sat, my hands in my lap, not moving or breathing.

The phone rang again, then stopped.

* * * * *

I had no tears.

But when it was finally over and the black limousine had driven Sylvia, Bessie and me to my apartment, the tears came.

And the cat, for no reason, jumped into my lap.

Chapter III

Alone now, I returned to the familiar routine that would get me through the days. Over the years I had build a protective wall that separated me from any but the most causal contact. Now, in my grief, I felt exposed, vulnerable, unable to handle the gestures of friendship that were so generously made. The wall, it seemed, was rebuilding itself without conscious help from me.

"If you don't snap out of this, I'll have you put away," Sylvia threatened. "Oh, darling, I do know what you're feeling. If I were to lose Bessie I would simply not be able to live!"

Bessie and Sylvia and I got along, were even comfortable as a threesome. And, as a threesome, we did spend time together. In the past it did not bother me when they openly showed their affection for each other but now I had to look away; the sight was too painful.

Finally, more months had passed since Candy's death than Candy and I had spent together. I worked, fed the cat, spent time with Sylvia and Bessie, took long drives and began to sleep through the night.

One difference, however. I moved into the smaller of the two bedrooms and the cat now slept at the foot of the bed.

Sylvia, returned from another honeymoon cruise with Bessie, called to invite me to a welcome home party she was giving for herself. "You're coming, and that's that," she stated. "Bessie will be hurt if you don't come and I will be furious. Really, Chris, you've spent enough time being sorry for yourself."

No one else would have dared to accuse me of self pity. But, then, I thought, no one else cares. Was I feeling sorry for myself?

"All right, Sylvia, I'll come to your party." Did these words have a familiar ring?

* * * * *

Sylvia's present was perfume in a crystal vase. She insisted that I pass it around so that everyone could sniff. Being the center of attention, if only for a few moments, embarrassed me. But, as I sat with my face getting red, I remembered that once I had promised myself to be happy.

After the perfume had made its way around the room I stoppered the vase and sat it on the piano by the music stand. Then I looked, actually looked, around the room at the faces. Some people I knew and they smiled or waved when our eyes met. Others were strangers to me but they nodded and raised their glass when I smiled at them.

"See," I told myself, "being happy isn't so hard." And I winked at Bessie who winked back.

Then I saw her.

During the years before Candy, I had seen women all over the place: women fully dressed, partially dressed, in bathing suits, naked or towel-wrapped in the steam room. Now, after having loved a woman and been loved by a woman, I had developed an appreciation for the female form. And the female face and form that I saw across the room literally took my breath away. I remembered Sylvia's words about the "perfect person" and I knew, without any doubts, that I was looking at that person now.

Her dress was black and simple with a tiny silver belt. Black shoes with very high heels raised her head about even with my chin. Her golden hair didn't quite touch her shoulders. She was laughing at something, her attention focused on someone in the group where she was standing.

I wanted her to turn her beautiful face to me and I projected that thought across the room. Concentrating. My eyes moved from her slender ankles to the hem of her dress; then my imagination carried me under the fabric to naked thighs and soft curves.

So there I stood, the dull tax attorney, leaning on Sylvia's piano and mentally undressing one of her female guests. My imagination was lingering on full breasts when Bessie appeared beside the woman, took her arm and, together, they crossed the room toward me.

Did Bessie notice that I was glassy eyed? Her little smile told me that she was indeed reading my mind, and her smile broadened as she said, "Chris, this is Meredith. You two have something in common, you're both into numbers." And, her look added, that's not all our Chris would like to be into . . .

There's a lot to be said for my composure. Being with Candy had given me enough self-assurance that I didn't stammer or choke. Outwardly, that is. With a calmness that belied my inner turmoil I managed to hold out my hand. Meredith's blue eyes looked into mine; her smile was nothing short of a miracle.

Is it possible to fall in love at first glance? I can't speak for anyone else but that's just what I did.

As we touched hands Meredith said the usual things and I think I replied with the usual things. Her hand was soft and warm and I wanted to hold it forever.

"What kind of numbers are yours?" Meredith asked as she withdrew her hand from mine.

"I do taxes." Why couldn't I think of anything else to say!

"Oh?" She was still smiling. "I teach math to tenth graders. Not as complicated as what you do. Where do you work?"

"In town." My mouth was as dry as a desert.

Meredith's smile was becoming fixed. I felt more awkward by the second and Bessie was enjoying it all tremendously. I had to say something or I'd lose her. "A drink," I stammered, "would you like a drink?" It wasn't until the words were out that I saw she had a full glass.

"Yes, I'd love one," she said calmly, and placed her glass on the piano next to the vase of perfume.

"You two have fun," said Bessie.

Meredith and I watched her weaving her way through the crowd toward Sylvia. Then Meredith turned back to me. "A drink, you said?"

I had gathered my wits. "Sure, the bar's this way." I took her arm.

* * * * *

I was determined to have Merry the instant I saw her at Sylvia's party. But neither Sylvia nor Bessie knew much about her and they couldn't answer my questions.

"Sweetheart, she is just the friend of a friend. She teaches. She does things with wildlife groups." Turning to Bessie, Sylvia asked the name of the clubs but Bessie didn't know. "And she either is or was married, I think."

The married part threw me for a minute but I took heart when Bessie, frowning as she tried to recall, said, "Was married. And someone told me that Merry had just moved into a new place and can walk to work ..."

"Sylvia, what am I going to do?" I was relieved that neither of them mentioned Candy. Were they wondering how I could turn away from mourning so quickly? It was a blessing to have understanding friends and both of them understanding the emotion motivating me.

"Let me see, now." Sylvia looked far into space. "I have it! We'll give a party, a small party, and invite Meredith."

The party was small, just the four of us. We sat around the heated pool, swam and ate catered barbecue.

Sylvia in a bathing suit is a sight to behold. She always had a perfect figure but the years since college had added softness. Not an ounce of fat, just rounded smoothness. Bessie was having a hard time keeping her hands from that glowing flesh.

I could appreciate Sylvia but I had been looking at her for years. Meredith was a different matter. On a scale of one to ten I gave Meredith a twenty to Sylvia's ten. Meredith was not trying to be provocative but I could not take my eyes from her.

I am adept at questioning people, I have to do it all the time in my work, so I deliberately kept Meredith talking about herself. She was flattered by the attention and, by afternoon, I probably knew more about her than she meant to tell.

Sipping my drink, listening to her halting phrases, I pieced together that her marriage had been a bomb from the very beginning. She had spent her wedding night alone in a hotel; he stayed drunk in a bar, booze apparently being more inviting than a new wife.

"So." She looked at me ruefully. "So, here I am, the virgin wife. I can't seem to get back to dating much anymore. Everyone tells me it takes time." She sighed and I watched the fabric of her suit strain against those soft mounds and the tiny straps stretch as she inhaled.

Over my suit I was wearing a terry cloth robe. Rising, I undid the belt and let the robe drop. Holding out my hand I said, "Let's swim, I need the exercise."

And swim we did. I found, to my surprise, that she was an excellent swimmer and almost more than a match for me. Our lazy splashing somehow became a race with Sylvia and Bessie shouting from the pool's edge.

I let her win, or at least I think I did. Bessie gallantly handed her a rose from the table and, for that, Sylvia pushed Bessie into the water then jumped in after her. Meredith and I watched them dunk each other at the shallow end.

We sat in a companionable silence, she thinking her thoughts and I thinking of making love to her. It was a lovely afternoon. Candy would have approved.

* * * * *

As the weeks passed, I made sure that we saw more and more of each other.

When I confessed to her that I had never learned the nine-times tables, she threatened to teach me. When she told me that the divorce had made her tax situation impossible, I offered to untangle it for her.

Her ten-year-old VW was often in the shop. My new Mercedes, the old one having been damaged beyond repair, had a roomy trunk just right for hauling tables and traverse rods for her apartment.

I helped her paint and paper her new apartment and I impressed her by caning two ancient chairs she bought at the Salvation Army store. She was always making curtains or painting walls or hanging pictures and her furniture was never in the same location twice. The apartment was small but bright and cozy. It was delightfully decorated and I felt more at home there than in my own place.

She was not broad-minded about gays. I think her husband was a closet case and I believe she thought the same.

"Remember, Sylvia and Bessie are gay," I reminded her one day when she made some remark about the "queers" at school.

"I know, but they're different."

"Different? In what way? A queer is a queer . . ." I was mocking her words.

"A rose by any other name, you mean?" She wrinkled her nose.

Suddenly disheartened, I just shook my head.

"Come on, Chris, I wasn't saying anything bad about Sylvia or Bessie. They're not queer, they're just . . . well, whatever. Anyway, I like them no matter what you call what they do."

"I don't want to call it anything, Merry; they're my friends and it's none of my business what they do." I was upset.

Merry touched my arm. "Please don't be angry, Chris. I'm sorry I said what I did. Forgive me?"

How could I not?

* * * * *

I told her that I thought I'd love camping, although I had never camped in my life. So we planned a weekend trip early in March. We checked wilderness trails and mileages and camping areas and made wildly various estimates of the amounts of food to take. We went together to buy the items she said I'd need. She already had her own well-used equipment and insisted that her VW was better for camping than my car. "The back seat folds down and we can store all of our things, okay?" I thought about my comfortable sedan with the huge trunk but then agreed that her tiny station wagon would be better.

I would have agreed to anything. My vision was of the two of us alone in the wilderness, sharing a sleeping bag. I planned somehow to lose hers so that we would be forced to sleep together in mine.

I was usually at her apartment two or three nights a week and often I stayed late. Once I felt that she was going to ask me to spend the night but something apparently changed her mind.

I knew I had a lot of groundwork to do before she might share any physical feelings but what a wonderful night if I could just have her next to me!

Chapter IV

Finally, late on a Friday afternoon, our camping weekend began. We packed and repacked Merry's VW station wagon. Most of the space was filled by our two bedrolls, a large ice chest, groceries, two folding chairs, the ground tarp, and Merry's pop-up tent. In addition to the jeans and shirts we were wearing, we had each packed a soft bag with an extra pair of jeans, walking shorts, a couple of shirts, socks to wear with boots, enough underclothing for three days and personal things like toothpaste and toothbrush. Merry had made a kind of sausage roll of two towels and one washcloth for each of us, plus a bar of soap, and this fitted neatly behind the seats.

Everything else was in a jumble, filling all the space we had. Laughing, I told her that what we needed was a trailer.

Hands on her hips, she surveyed the small butane stove that wouldn't fit. "Maybe we should just spend the weekend in a motel," she suggested, "and take walks around the parking lot."

Privately, I liked that idea but didn't say so aloud. I leaned on the hood and watched as she walked around the little car, peering through the glass, a cloth travel bag filled with field guides in one hand and our hiking boots dangling from the other, and binoculars around her neck. It was a moment filled with joy for me. We were going to be together, alone, for an entire weekend, no phones, no interruptions.

Even without encouragement from Merry, my love for her had grown to the point where I found it increasingly difficult to maintain my "straight" pose. Recently there had been happy moments that called for closeness and we had hugged each other spontaneously. Merry, however, was always first to drop her arms and move away. Nevertheless, I felt an excitement about this weekend; an almost breathless feeling that something was going to happen between us.

So I smiled and joked as we tugged things out onto the ground and began repacking until we had everything fitted into the folded-down back seat area. My good spirits were contagious and Merry shouted in triumph when the motor finally caught and, with a cloud of black smoke, we were on our way.

It was Merry's plan to camp near the hiking trail. The place she had selected was at a kind of crossroads where several trails radiated out from a densely wooded area. She parked the VW on an abandoned road that ended something less than a mile from the place where we planned to camp.

"You mean we have to carry all this stuff for a mile!" I was aghast. "We'll have to make a dozen trips!"

"Don't complain, Chris, or I'll make you eat all your food raw." She had promised to do the cooking so this was a serious threat.

The light was fast fading from the sky. "Should we be wandering around in the woods so late?" I asked. "How will we find our way?"

"With your new flashlight, of course."

"My new flashlight?" I asked stupidly. "Merry," I almost shouted, "I forgot to bring it!"

"Oh." A wry little smile formed as she thought about that for a moment. "Guess you're in luck then. We'll stay here until morning and then move our things."

"Where will we sleep?" I looked around at what little I could see of the deserted road that was hardly more than a gravel path overrun with weeds, not very inviting. The wind had picked up since we'd parked and it was getting chilly. I could see the silhouetted shapes of trees close to the roadside beginning to shake as the gusts hit them.

Merry pointed to a slight rise. "We'll camp in the shelter of those trees so we can have a fire protected from the wind. I'll make some coffee." She poked my arm with her fist. "Cheer up, girl scout, we'll be cozy and comfy in no time."

She rooted through our gear and pulled out her sleeping bag, the camp stove, some groceries and the sack of cooking utensils. "Grab whatever you can, Chris." As she moved away from me, she called over her shoulder, "Isn't this great!"

It was great to be alone with her, yes, but the motel would have been more comfortable. I grabbed my sleeping bag, some cigarettes, pulled out the ground tarp and both folding chairs, and followed Merry through the weeds. Then I went back for the ice chest and again for the tent.

After a few minutes of being very busy, she had the water bubbling on the stove and another crackling fire burning on the ground near us. I could clearly see her face in the fire's glow. She was sitting with her hands clasped around her knees, looking very much at home.

"You handle this like you'd been a pioneer all your life."

She looked at me, obviously pleased. "I love being out in the open. I think I'd rather camp than anything else."

I thought of several things I'd rather do with her but for now I was content just to be this near.

We arranged our sleeping bags next to each other, had strong, black coffee to sip and dried fruit to nibble as we watched the fire.

I thought how little I actually knew about this woman whom I had grown to love so very much. I was happy that she had spent so much of her time with me since our meeting at Sylvia's. Happy, yet uncertain why she had chosen me as a companion. The nine or ten years difference in our age was not that great but she had many opportunities to mingle with her co-workers, participating in school related activities with people who shared her interests.

I wondered if she felt safe with me . . . not safe in the physical sense but safe in that she was coasting, accepting a friendship that demanded little of her while she rebuilt her defenses after her disastrous marriage.

Did she suspect that I was a lesbian? Could she know that I had fallen totally in love with her? I did not think that I had ever shown my feelings, acting only the part of a somewhat more than casual friend.

Watching her as she stared into the fire, I became strangely sad. Since the beginning I had hoped that one day I could tell her that I was in love with her — perhaps even this weekend — and I hoped she could love me in return. I had little experience in this kind of thing but I imagined that the time we spent together would form a bond that could turn to love if I told her my feelings. Tonight, watching her and remembering her derisive comments about "queers," I began to feel that it was probably a lost cause. She had never shown any sign that her friendship for me could ever grow into more than the affection one woman friend can have for another.

What if hearing of my love should cause her to turn from me in disgust? She would see me as just another "queer." I knew I couldn't stand that. What I should do was stop loving her, cancel her from my life and find someone who would love me without restrictions, another woman who could share her life with me. My best move was to stand by Sylvia's piano until another "perfect woman" appeared.

"Why are you so sad, Chris?" Merry reached over to me. "Is anything wrong?"

I looked at her beautiful face and saw the concern in her eyes. "No, nothing. I was just thinking . . . staring into the fire."

"For a minute you looked like you'd just lost your best friend."

"Nothing like that." I forced a smile and, satisfied, she smiled back.

We sat for a few more minutes, both lost in our private thoughts. When the first few drops of rain hit the fire, I became aware that the wind had become very strong and there were flashes of lightning crackling in the distance.

"Hey," Merry said, "looks like we're in for a storm."

"What'll we do?" I asked, feeling the back of my shirt already wet.

"Come on, let's go to the car!" Merry emptied the coffee pot, grabbed up her sleeping bag and started running for the road. I was right behind her, my bag dragging through the weeds.

We crowded into the front seats, shoving our bags behind us. We were both wet, the rain was now a driving force, the drops hitting the car like little bombs.

"Wow! The paper didn't say anything about rain. It was supposed to be clear and sunny all weekend." She wiped her face on her sleeve. "When this lets up I'll fix your supper ... if everything hasn't washed away. It's a good thing we stayed near the car!"

I couldn't help but agree. I wanted a cigarette but my pack was on the ground by the fire and my spare packs were somewhere under everything else in the back of the car.

"Guess we'll just have to wait it out!"

"Do we have a choice?" I asked.

The thunder was so loud that we were shouting to make ourselves heard. Lightning flashed closer and closer until the sky was so bright we could have counted the blades of grass if the windshield hadn't been frosted.

We huddled, each in our bucket seat, feeling the car shudder as the wind slammed into it. I reached for my sleeping bag and put it around my shoulders. It was some comfort from the cold that suddenly filled the car. I helped Merry drape her own bag around her shoulders and arms.

"Merry, are you as cold as I am?" I shouted.

"This is really weird, isn't it? I'm about to freeze!" She clutched her bag tighter.

I was frightened. The lightning was hitting the earth all around us with tremendous sound. Flash after flash crashed so near I could have reached out and caught some. We were deafened by the sound. The air had an odor like electric wires sparking.

"Don't worry, Merry," I yelled, "we're in a car with tires that insulate us from the ground. Even if it hits us, we won't be hurt!"

I had read this somewhere and fervently hoped it was true. To make a liar out of me, a bolt of blue-white fire danced its way from the hood, across the roof, then off the back of the car. It was instantly followed by another, then another, and I felt myself sizzle. It was not like being electrocuted, but it probably came close.

The light inside the car was so bright that I had to close my eyes. Even through closed lids the brightness was so unbearable I covered my eyes with my hands.

I could hear Merry shouting, or crying, but the noise was so great that my ears refused to hear any sound but the crackling and crashing of the lightning bolts as the little car actually danced up and down on the road.

On and on went this assault on our senses; the fiery light and the thunderous noise. There was no doubt in my mind that we were directly in the center of whatever was happening.

We were both huddled in our seats, Merry leaning on the steering wheel with her arms wrapped around her head and me crouched as low as I could in my seat, knees drawn up and my head pillowed on them.

The car shuddered and jerked as one tremendous bolt after another lit on it and next to it. Then, like a horse rearing, the VW flew into the air, turned on its side and dove toward the earth.

The turning motion made my head fly back and smack into the door post, causing stars to flash inside my head that were far brighter than those in the heavens and I think it hurt, but before I could form the thought, my head snapped forward and something equally hard smashed into my face. Those bright stars dimmed, then disappeared.

I seemed to be drifting in a place that was warm and quiet. There were beautiful colors floating before my eyes like gossamer banners drifting on a gentle breeze. How lovely!

This idyll was interrupted by someone calling my name. I tried not to listen but the person began jerking my arm and calling louder.

"Chris, please!" More jerking. "Chris, look at me!" Frantic jerking.

I opened one eye (what was wrong with the other?) and peered at the person. For some reason I could not speak.

"Help me, Chris! Please help!" The steady pull on my arm threatened to lift me from my seat. "Chris, you have to get out! Come on, stand, damn it!"

With as much strength as I could find, I unscrambled my legs and stood. Was there something wrong with the car? Dimly I perceived that I was standing on the inside of one door with my head poking out the other door which was open to the sky. Was the car on its side, I wondered? I could not decide.

Who was this person whose arms were under mine, yanking on me, and why was this person yelling in my ear?

"Help me, Chris, stand on the edge of the seat and push!"

I stood on the side of the seat and put my elbows over the door sill and heaved myself upwards. This was more effort than I wanted to exert but maybe it would make the person hush and leave me alone. The colored banners were returning and I felt myself relaxing. Good!

No, not so good. The infuriating person still clutched me under both arms and was yanking harder. Now I was leaning on my stomach, half in and half out of the car; my feet and legs inside, my head and arms hanging over the bottom of the car. How was this possible? Again, I couldn't decide.

I felt another huge heave under my arms and my body cleared the opening. The momentum caused me to crash, head first, into the person who had caused all of this, both of us falling to the ground. Then the lovely colored banners returned. Good!

* * * * *

Slowly, I became aware of activity and sound. Merry was dabbing at my face with a wet cloth, babbling, tears streaming down her face. I peered at her cautiously through one eye.

"I had to get you out of the car," she was saying, "I didn't mean to hurt you but the gas was leaking all over the place and the battery was pouring acid all over the seat . . ."

Between sobs, Merry was explaining something to me but none of it made any sense. The cool cloth felt good on my forehead, but when she touched my nose, the stars reappeared, then dimmed and went dark.

Chapter V

If I noticed anything at all, it was the absence of noise.

"Whad happed?" I croaked at Merry, seeing her sitting on the ground next to me. She lifted her head and the joy on her face would have made me deliriously happy any other time.

Taking my hand, she leaned over me. "Thank God you're all right. I've been so worried." She began to cry.

"Doad cry, Berry. I'b okay." Were those words mine? I realized that I was breathing through my mouth. I made an effort to breathe through my nose but no air came through.

"By doze, whads wrog?" I could hardly understand myself. I squeezed her hand, questioning with my eyebrows.

Choking back sobs, she told me that she had hit my face with the back of her head when the car pitched forward. That I now had a black eye and, if my nose wasn't broken, at least it was badly bent.

"You have a horrible lump on the back of your head, too." She sniffed, her eyes still brimming. "I thought yesterday that your skull was cracked."

"Whed?" She had said yesterday, hadn't she?

"This is Sunday morning, Chris."

I closed my eyes to take all of this in. It felt good to have them closed. I drifted.

The next time I opened my eyes, I found myself sitting, propped against a tree and wrapped in a warm, soft sleeping bag. I could tell I was not clothed.

Merry, the cheerfulness not so forced now, was stirring something in one of the tiny pots, looking expectantly at me. "Think you can eat now?" She held out a spoonful of whatever it was. I had to go by sight because there was no way I could smell.

"Whad id it?" Sight alone was not enough.

"I've made you some soup. You need to get your strength back."

Try eating with a clothespin on your nose. Can't taste, can't breathe, can't swallow. Merry kept putting the spoon to my mouth and when I got some of it down I did feel better. The headache I had would probably be with me forever from the feel of it but that was not an immediate problem. What Merry was saying, was.

". . . so I've looked around and it's truly not the same," she said. "I haven't been far because I didn't want to leave you but the little I've seen . . ." She looked at me so seriously that I knew she wanted me to say something, or worse, to do something.

The only words that sank in were "not the same" and I had no idea what it was that wasn't the same.

"We have to do something, Chris!"

My worst fears realized, I pushed the spoon away. Sliding deeper into the sleeping bag, I told her, "Berry, toborrow, I'll thig aboud it toborrow, okay?"

* * * * *

Tomorrow, when I woke, I was still in the bag but wearing only briefs and a shirt. I was clean and dry and sweet-smelling like a baby. Merry had been busy while I slept. She was at my side instantly when I stirred.

"Are you feeling any better?"

I nodded. My head still throbbed but some air was coming through my nose. I could see with both eyes, too. The swelling that had almost closed my left eye had gone down.

"Well, then." She was going to be cheerful if it killed her. "Here's some coffee to start your day."

Sitting up, I held the cup myself while I sipped the delicious brew. As I drank, we smiled at each other. "Now," I said when the cup was empty, "what's this that isn't the same?"

The cheer dropped from her face, her eyes widened. "This place isn't, that's what. We're not in the same place we were when the storm started Friday night. We're in a different place. Nothing is the same . . . the trees, there's no road, there are mountains all around . . ." She rushed breathlessly through a recitation that sounded as if she'd practiced it many times.

My jaw had dropped. At the look on my face she started again, "It's not the same, Chris. There're mountains and no sign of people and . . ."

I stopped her. "Merry, slow down. Now, what is it you're telling me?"

"I'm telling you," she began carefully, "that we have somehow moved to another place." She pulled the map out of her shirt pocket. "See?" She pointed to a spot, one we had circled with yellow marker. "See, we're supposed to be here but we're not here. We're someplace else."

That bash on my head must have dulled my wits. I simply could not make any sense out of what Merry was saying. Trying to assemble logical possibilities, I took in a deep breath, through my mouth because I didn't trust my nose. "Wait, Merry. Start over and tell me what you're talking about."

Clutching the map to her chest, she began slowly, tremulously, "Do you remember the lightning storm?"

I nodded.

"Well, the car turned on its side and all the gas spilled out and I was afraid the lightning would make the car explode." She looked at me for affirmation.

Yes, again, I would have had the same fear.

"So I pulled you out of the car, grabbed the sleeping bags and we started moving away. When you couldn't walk any more we stopped." She pointed to some trees. "Over there. At first I was afraid to be under trees but the lightning seemed to be only where the car was so we stayed there all night. You were out of it, but I watched . . ."

I could follow that part of the story. On Saturday, according to Merry, the storm was over and she moved me (apparently I walked when forced to) and made me comfortable. Then she emptied the car of what was left of our camping gear.

It rained in the morning and she had made a sort of tent out of her sleeping bag to keep the water off me. She ate but I wouldn't. Saturday was cool but Sunday was bright and clear and warm.

I had soiled my clothes and sleeping bag but Merry heated water in our tiny pot, bathed me and washed the clothes and sleeping bag in a little clear running stream that had appeared where no stream had been on Friday.

Sunday I slept, off and on, all day. Merry was frightened because she could see that we were not in the place where we had camped Friday night but her concern was with me. In the afternoon she realized that watching me sleep wasn't helping so she collected wood and built a huge signal fire that sent up billows of black smoke.

Later, seeing that I was comfortable and sleeping peacefully, she climbed a steep hill that was sitting directly over the spot where we had started to camp on Friday night. Looking in all directions she recognized nothing that was shown on the map.

The hill was rocky and we had seen no rocky hills on Friday. The gully and the stream were new. The distant mountains were new, the nearby hills were new. There was no sign of human habitation for as far as her bird-watching binoculars could see. Wherever we were, it wasn't the place where we'd stopped on Friday.

The more she looked the stranger everything appeared. She had poked about a bit then returned to me. She kept a roaring fire going all last night as protection from whatever. Yesterday she had tried to tell me but I had not responded.

Today, I responded. Believing, yet not believing, I struggled out of the bag. "Let's go take a look." Merry handed me my jeans, tennis shoes and clean socks and, sitting cross-legged on the ground, watched me as I dressed.

We walked across a clearing, climbed into and out of the gully, waded through the stream, passing the VW on the way, and stood looking up at the wall that faced us.

"How did you climb it?" It was so high and straight up that I knew only wings could get us to the top.

"Over there where that big piece broke off, there's a sort of incline."

A huge section, as big as a four-story building, had broken away from the cliff face and made a perfect ramp to within a foot of the top.

We climbed, with some effort on my part, and when I stood on the flat, nearly treeless top I understood what Merry had been telling me. Looking in all directions I saw nothing but trees and mountains. Trees and hills close up, but farther away on the horizon, mountains. The mountains were huge and, even from this distance, unbelievably high with snow covering the jagged upper heights.

There were no snow-covered mountains where we lived. On this entire continent there were no mountains like the ones I saw. We were standing on a kind of ridge, in a tree-covered valley that stretched for miles and miles until the mountains almost filled the sky on all sides. And, for all of those miles and miles, there was nothing but trees. As far as I could see, nothing but trees and hills and mountains. No sign of human habitation, not in any direction. I saw no line of wire-covered poles stretching into infinity, no smoke belching from factory stacks, no jet trails in the clear blue sky, not an interstate highway or a plowed field.

Were we in Tibet? It was the only place I could think of that may have had a landscape like the one I saw. Something told me that we were not in Tibet.

Merry was clutching my arm, making it hard to focus the glasses. She was frightened.

"See, what did I tell you?"

I lowered the glasses and looked at her. I had no clever words. I opened my mouth and what came out was, "Merry, where the hell are we?"

Chapter VI

After coming down from the cliff, we sat under our tree and very soberly discussed our situation.

We came to few conclusions. We had some options though. We could gather up what camping gear and food we had and start hiking. But hiking in which direction? There were mountains all around us and no sign of human activity. How to guess which way to hike? Merry estimated a couple of days' hike just to get to the foothills. Then what? And, was there more of the same on the other side of the mountains?

We could, of course, stay where we were, keep signal fires going and wait for someone to see and investigate.

Then there was the problem of food. We still had some dried fruit, a few packages of trail food, some coffee, sugar, powdered cream and half a dozen candy bars. My cigarettes had been eaten by the acid.

Fortunately, the weather was on our side. It was, after all, early spring. Although it felt colder than it should be for this time of year, we would have good weather for a while. But good weather for what?

Our options, then, were actually only two. Go or stay.

To go meant facing unknown hardships and the possibility that we would find no one.

To stay meant facing unknown hardships and the possibility that no one would find us.

Neither of us was ready at that moment to examine the whys and the wherefores of our being transported here, wherever "here" was and if "transported" was the word. Merry had been aware of the "problem," as she called it, for a longer time and had no explanation so I didn't feel obliged to offer one, even if I had something in mind, which I didn't. We were both in shock. Neither of us knew any more than the other and so, by unspoken consent, we just didn't talk about it in depth. Not that day, anyway.

Merry thought, and I agreed, that the car, a bright red, had a good chance of being spotted from the air. Except for the cliff, the immediate area was relatively flat, there was clean running water, and the cliff top had only a few clumps of trees so that we could keep a signal fire going without danger of setting any woods on fire.

Eventually, someone had to find us. My staff would set up a hue and cry and Sylvia would alert every able-bodied person in the country to begin a search. Probably by air, sea and land, if I knew Sylvia.

In addition to the wildness of the area there was a strangeness that I couldn't put a name to. There were trees and foliage that simply didn't look right. Merry put a name to it. "This place looks like it's a grade B sci-fi movie set," she said.

With that thought in mind I took a really good look around and then told her I agreed with her. "Maybe we're both dreaming and when we wake up we'll be home in bed." I smiled to show that I didn't exactly mean in bed together but Merry hadn't taken it that way, anyway.

After we'd been there five days without a sign of anyone coming for us, not even the distant drone of an aircraft, I had a distinctly uneasy feeling that we had better consider preparing ourselves for heavy weather because, when cold weather came, we were probably going to be right here in the same place we found ourselves now. The gleaming snow on the mountains had convinced me that winter in this place would be very white.

I did not communicate this change of feeling to Merry because I did not want to destroy her hopes. We could be rescued at any time, couldn't we? There was always that possibility, however remote as it began to seem to me.

Our food supply had been meant for a few days and we had already eaten most of it. When that was gone, what then? And shelter. If we weren't rescued almost immediately we would need shelter from the rain and sun and night.

I took stock of our tools and became very discouraged. Each of us wore a small sheath knife attached to our belt; we had one sharpening stone, one all-metal hatchet, a tire tool that was flattened on one end like a pry bar, an axle jack that probably wouldn't be of much use in carpentry, a long phillips screwdriver, a short-handled regular screwdriver and one rusty pair of pliers from under the VW seat. Also, two forks, two knives, four spoons. Without hammer, nails, or saw, it might be possible to build the kind of shelter where everything leaned on everything else, like a tepee ... but where to build it?

"Maybe on top of the cliff," Merry suggested. "Let's go look up there again."

I labored up the ramp behind Merry to the same place we had seen already. The area was flat but the wind was brisk. Probably too unprotected to build there.

Merry asked with a frown, "What about the bottom of the cliff?"

So we went down, much easier than going up. We surveyed the gently sloping are at the foot of the cliff. At least we would have one wall of our shelter already built.

"Chris, let's build here."

I agreed, carefully nodding my aching head.

Now that we had made our great decision, I said to Merry, "You know about wilderness shelter, what do we do first?"

"I have no idea." She shrugged helplessly. "I usually had a tent."

This caught me up short for a second and I sighed. "Well, we'll just have to learn together, I guess." I wasn't too optimistic but was anxious to get started with whatever it was that we were going to build. My head was still pounding so hard that I felt cross-eyed and the sooner I had a place to lie down, the better.

We stumbled upon what was to become our home while climbing the incline to the cliff top. Loaded with wood, we were about half way up the ramp when Merry slipped on some loose gravel and fell back into me. We both sat down hard and, while we were untangling ourselves and the wood, happened to move aside a thick clump of vines growing on the cliff face.

When the chunk of stone on which we were climbing had broken away from the larger mass, it had exposed a slotted opening in the cliff face. There had probably been a tunnel in the fallen portion that led to the large opening which we now saw partially covered by greenery.

"Think a bear lives there?" Merry asked in a whisper.

"No," I whispered back, "look at the spider webs."

The opening, after we cleared away some of the vines, was slightly wider than an ordinary door and festooned with cobwebs which were gently moving in a breeze that seemed to come from inside the opening.

"Can we go in?" Merry asked, pushing me from behind.

"When you put it that way, sure." I moved forward cautiously, waving aside cobwebs with the stout stick in my hand.

When I came to the larger opening I stopped, causing Merry to walk into me. I enjoyed feeling us touch even if only back to front. It occurred to me in that instant that if I had turned around and bent my head an inch or two and if she had looked up at me, we would have found our lips touching. Merry hadn't noticed, however, so I moved a few steps into darkness, peering cautiously around me.

I was staring into gloom. Turning to Merry, I said, "Hey, we'll need a torch to go any farther." I was excited about our discovery. We had found a cave, a real live cave and it looked unoccupied!

Near the VW we hurriedly made two torches from slender branches wrapped with a moss-like substance which Merry found and rubbed in the oil that had spilled from the VW. This homemade contraption burned slowly and brightly, giving off much black smoke. My cigarette lighter, still full of fluid, lit the torches for us.

Back at the entrance, almost tiptoeing, we moved slowly into the cave. The entranceway sloped slightly, the "hallway" measuring about six feet long and something wider than a door. A few steps and we were standing in a high-ceilinged room that was sort of rectangular, about twenty-five feet long and sixteen feet wide, more or less.

Our torchlight reached all corners. The floor sloped slightly to the outside, and was rough, and littered with leaves and loose stones. The walls were not exactly at right angles with the floor and the cathedral ceiling arched into blackness overhead but this was definitely a "room." The slight musty odor was not unpleasant and there was a faint breeze, soft and steady, coming from somewhere.

Merry clutched my arm, her torch held high over her head. "Do you think we can camp in here tonight?" she asked, awed.

I grinned at her, ignoring the pain this caused my nose and very pleased to think of all the work we wouldn't have to do. "Yep, padnuh, this here'll be it!" I tipped my imaginary hat forward and hooked a thumb in my gun belt. "Rekon this'll be jest fine."

My response got the smile I hoped for. Merry squeezed my elbow, her eyes alight. At that instant we were both pretending that this was some kind of exciting adventure that we could walk away from when we tired of it.

We began moving in immediately. "Moving in" meant hauling up the incline and into the cave our sleeping bags, pillows, the two bags with extra clothing, our towels, the two aluminum cooking pots and two aluminum plates, our coffee pot, the tools and the remainder of our food. We also gathered fallen limbs, as many as we could carry in five or six loads, and stacked them at the far end of the room. Having no broom, we used leafy branches and our feet to sweep aside some of the loose stuff on the floor so we could place our sleeping bags on a fairly level place.

We filled our two canteens with fresh water from the creek and, using rocks, we built a fire pit, both to keep us warm in the chilly night and for cooking.

Cooking *what* was the problem.

"If we're not found soon we're going to have to do something about food," I told Merry that night. We were going to bed hungry, trying to save something for the next day.

"Do what?" she asked, her eyes huge in the firelight. We were sitting, propped against the wall sipping coffee and watching bright sparks fly towards the ceiling. Merry had drawn herself into a tight ball, arms wrapped around her blue-jeaned legs, her chin resting on her knees. She was discouraged; we had both watched the sky for days and seen nothing, heard nothing. "How long do you think it'll take, Chris?"

I knew what she meant. "Oh, I don't know." And I really didn't. "We'll probably be picked up sooner or later." That seemed to be a safe thing to say although I didn't believe a word of it and, as it turned out, neither did she.

There was a deep, chilling fear inside me. To stop the trembling of my hands I clutched the tin cup, the heat of the liquid unnoticed. Any reserve of courage I may have possessed was fast disappearing. My head throbbed, my nose felt like it was full of wet cotton, I had a stiff neck, and I was hungry, uncomfortable, and desperately tired. I wanted only to put my head on Merry's soft breasts and sink into unconsciousness.

I must have sighed aloud because Merry turned to me. Her voice was pleading, low, almost a whisper. "Chris, I need for you to be strong."

I stared at her. A voice inside my head told me that now it would be all right to go to her and take her in my arms but, alas, my arms were too heavy to lift.

So I simply said, "I will be, Merry." And I knew I would or I'd die trying.

It was pitch dark outside so, our coffee finished, we said goodnight and snuggled down in our bed roll on the hard rock floor. The room was still fire-lit and we watched the embers slowly fade, though we did not talk.

Lying there I remembered the night of our camping trip and how I had stared into the fire then, too, and that I had thought of cancelling her out of my life, of not loving her anymore. Now I knew that I could not turn off my feelings. I loved her. I loved her deeply and forever. If we could not be lovers then I would be everything else that she wanted; I would somehow give her the strength she needed.

It was almost funny. Here I was, finally, sleeping only inches away from Merry but I might as well have been alone. I had been alone before Candy, not even knowing that I was. It's better not to know, I thought. At least not knowing didn't hurt.

Sighing, I pulled my cover up over my ears and slept.

During the night, when things were very still and our room was in total darkness I woke and heard water. Running water, not a drip. And yet we had not seen water when we explored earlier. I tried to place the sound but it seemed to come from all over.

At daylight I put more wood in our fire pit, relit the fire and put water on to heat for coffee. Squatting there, I looked around carefully. Faint sunlight was coming in the opening, and the fire, once it caught, burned brightly, casting a cheerful glow on the walls. Our door faced east and the sun, when slightly higher, would shine almost directly into our room. I listened for the water sound, turning my head this way and that, but couldn't hear it clearly.

Gingerly, I felt the lump on the back of my head. It seemed not as big as yesterday and not quite as painful. It would be nice to wash my hair, I thought, and even nicer to have a hot bath. I couldn't remember ever going to bed fully clothed, in my not-too-clean shirt and jeans, as we had been doing. I thought to wake Merry but she was still sound asleep, unmoving, not even her nose showing. So, using a towel to protect my hand, I lifted the pot from the fire, poured my cup full of steaming water, added a few crystals of coffee and a pinch of sugar. I enjoyed the coffee aroma that filled my nose. How lovely to be able to smell again!

As I sat there, sipping, I watched the shadows moving on the wall as the direction of the light changed. And then I saw it. To my left there was another opening. It was smaller than our "front door" and, even as I stood and walked over to it, it almost disappeared from sight.

What we thought was a natural protrusion of stone was actually a thin pillar that stood out from the wall and hid the opening behind it. I stood and looked into the dark opening, the sound of water now very clear.

"Chris?" Merry had awakened. She was propped up on her elbows. "What are you doing?"

"Come take a look!"

Together, with the aid of a torch, we explored. The opening led directly into another room. It was narrow and not more than ten feet long but this ceiling, too, arched up into total darkness. At the farther end was a stream of water about thirty inches deep, a dirty, yellowish brown color with leaves and twigs in abundance. The water appeared from under the right side wall, rushed through a trough that it had worn over the years and then disappeared into the other wall.

"This can be our bathroom," Merry breathed.

So we now had a cold water flat.

* * * * *

After a breakfast of dried fruit and coffee, we tidied the area where we had slept, made sure the smoldering embers were confined to the fire pit and in no danger of spreading, then climbed the ramp to the top of the cliff. It seemed an easier climb for me than yesterday but, truthfully, not easy enough. The last few steps were difficult.

"Think we should build a smoky fire, Chris?"

"Um, yeah. If we want to be found, I guess we'd better. We'll have to go down to the woods to get more stuff to burn, though. What's left here won't last long at all." Remembering the million trips we had made up the ramp with wood yesterday, I almost groaned aloud.

Merry had been searching the horizon but now turned to me. "You don't look too perky. I think what you should do is sit someplace in the shade and rest. Let me get the wood, okay?"

"No, indeed. I feel perfectly all right. Anyway, we can get it done faster if we work together."

"Chris, we don't have any reason to do it fast. Come on, now . . ." And she took my arm and led me to a windblown clump of trees on the far edge of the cliff. "I think you'd be more comfortable in the cave but I'll bring a pillow and you can look after the fire and rest at the same time."

I started to protest but her look was so stern that I laughed instead. "I just got out of resting in bed all night. There's nothing wrong with me, honest, I'm okay." Maybe not quite the truth but close enough.

"Hush! I'm going to bring another cup of coffee, your pillow and the foraging book and you will rest and read and look after the fire. How's that sound?"

I picked a shady spot, brushed it clear, and sat. "It sounds fine. I'll sit for a while but when I get up you're not to fuss at me. I can't let you do everything, I have to do my share."

"Pooh." But she was grinning as she turned away. I watched her walk to the edge then seemingly step off into thin air. She turned and waved but then disappeared before I could respond. I settled my back against the rough tree bark and closed my eyes. That damned headache was still pounding away and my nose was aching. How I wished I felt better! A hot bath and a couple of aspirins would do just fine right now . . .

I jerked awake when I felt a hand on my forehead. Merry was kneeling next to me. "You have a fever, Chris," she said softly. "Let's go back to the cave where it's cooler."

Completely disoriented, I got to my feet. "What . . ."

Merry put her arm around my waist. "Lean on me," she said. I did. More because it felt good than for support. Very carefully she led me down the ramp to our cave. She was right, it was cooler and darker and my sleeping bag was soft around me. The damp cloth on my head was good, too. I slept again.

It was late afternoon when I woke, thirsty and ravenously hungry. I looked around for Merry but she was not in the cave. I found my shoes where she had put them and was almost out the door when I met her coming in.

"What are you doing up?"

"Looking for you."

She put her hand on my forehead. Relief evident in her voice, she said, "The fever's gone, thank goodness. How do you feel?"

"I feel absolutely fine. Good enough to haul my share of the wood now."

"No!"

"No? Why not?"

"Because I said so. Anyway, we're going to eat. I've brought some water for you to wash your face and hands so go sit." She pointed to a log by the fire pit.

"Yes, ma'am." I sat on the log and washed, then Merry served watery soup, our last package, I think, and something new.

"How is it?" she asked after I took my first taste of her surprise.

"It's good. Tastes like spinach. No, like mustard greens." I couldn't decide which. "Where'd you find this?"

"In the shallow water by the stream. I've seen ducks in the park eat green leaves and they didn't die so I thought we'd probably survive, too, especially if I boiled them. Anyway, we're almost out of everything else."

I scraped my bowl to get the last bite. "Do we get dessert?"

"You bet! How does chocolate sound?"

We each had half a bar and we ate slowly, savoring the rich taste. When we had swallowed the last bite, Merry handed me the damp cloth. "Wipe your hands then get back in bed. And stay there." She picked up the dishes and pots and utensils. "I'm going to the stream to wash these. You be asleep when I get back . . . or else!"

I started to ask her what the "or else" would be but instead I said, "Be careful, Merry. Don't be gone too long."

I was going to stay awake to tell her about the foraging course I had taken so many lifetimes ago but I was full and sleepy and so I slept.

* * * * *

It was Merry's idea to form a huge SOS on the cliff top. So the next day, in spite of Merry's objections, I worked with her for many tiresome hours hauling rocks to use in making the letters. Finally, satisfied that our design was legible should a high-flying plane cross our valley, Merry decided that we had done all we could to aid in our rescue.

"Some things that were so simple aren't simple any more," she stated as we walked down-ramp.

"Like what?"

"Food, for one. It was always so easy to run to the market. I never gave a thought to how the food got there, did you?"

"Can't say that I did."

"You know that we're out of food, don't you? We haven't anything to eat but the greens." She sniffed and leaned to wipe her face on her shirt tail, leaving a brown smudge on her cheek.

"Yes, I knew that and are you catching a cold, Merry?" We had reached our cave.

"No, I'm just hot from carrying all those rocks. Makes my nose run." And she wrinkled her nose at me. "Wish I had some Kleenex."

"I wish I had a bath! I haven't done anything but dab at myself for a week and I'm beginning to rot, I think."

"Well, for goodness sake! We have a perfect swimming hole right outside our door. Come on, let's go bathe in the stream!" And before I could say anything she had snatched the soap and two towels and was pulling me out the door.

We were running by the time we reached the water. Merry threw her clothes and shoes behind her on the bank and waded to the middle of the wonderful, clear-flowing stream.

I was a little slower, mostly from shyness, but the water looked so cool and clean that I heaved my clothes on the bank too, then took a cautious step forward. The water at its deepest just reached my knees. Both of us sat at the same time. I ducked my head and came up shuddering. "Damn, it's cold, Merry!"

"Oh, you sissy! It feels great!" And to prove it she leaned back on her arms and began kicking her feet, showering me. I caught her ankles and held them as she struggled. We played like children, screaming and sputtering and splashing each other. I was acutely conscious of our nakedness, and as we grabbed each other in play I felt her hand touch my breasts, her arm circle my waist. It was almost a relief to begin the serious business of washing hair and body. We even washed our clothes.

Later, squeaky clean and towel-wrapped we sat on the floor of our cave and drank coffee. We both felt renewed. There's something about being clean that makes other things bearable.

"We should have thought about that stream days ago, Chris. Tomorrow morning I'm going to wash all of our dirty clothes." She drained her cup. "Won't it feel good to have clean clothes?"

"I like clean clothes. I like clean hair. I'd like a steak and a baked potato with bacon chips and sour cream and butter and chives . . . but I'll settle for boiled greens and coffee. That is what our supper's going to be, isn't it?"

"Yep. At least it will be if we go collect the greens."

I sighed aloud at the thought.

"Would you rather stay here?" Merry was suddenly serious and concerned. "I can go pick greens without you, you know. Maybe you'd better cool it for another day or so, till your head is better."

"My head's better just from being clean." I stood and tightened the towel securely around my body. "Let's go, Lady Godiva, I'm hungry."

* * * * *

It was Merry's idea to copy my tiny wallet calendar onto notebook paper we'd found in the VW glove compartment. We weren't sure what month or day it was in this place so we began the calendar on March fifteenth, the day we started our camping trip. Each morning we'd cross off one more day. There were eight days crossed out already when I fell asleep that night.

Chapter VII

"Chris!" Merry's hand was shaking my shoulder. "Wake up!"

Eyes open, I peered up at her. I hoped it wasn't morning but the fact that I could see her face meant that it was well into daylight already. How had I slept so late?

"I saw fish in the stream, Chris! Big ones! We have to catch them!" She was breathless from running up the ramp.

Too groggy to comprehend, I echoed, "Catch them?"

Merry sat back on her heels. "They're this big . . ." She measured with her hands. "And there may be some even bigger!"

"Okay, I'm up." It was a struggle to get my head off the pillow but with Merry's help unzipping my bed, I managed to sit, feeling slightly embarrassed because of my nakedness.

"I didn't want to wake you because you needed the rest but I had to tell you about the fish." She handed me clean dry clothes from yesterday and my socks and shoes. I dressed fast then ran my fingers through my hair, yawning widely.

"Are you feeling better this morning?"

"Umm, I think so. At least my head doesn't hurt." I was somewhat surprised to discover that my nose was clear, too. "I think I'll probably live."

"I'm so glad, Chris. It's been awful, not having anything to give you for the pain." She reached and gently touched my cheek. "The swelling is mostly gone and your eye is more yellow than black." Her fingers were light as she cupped my face, searching for signs of improvement. "I'll never forgive myself for doing this to you!"

"Don't say that, Merry. I'm really okay, just uglier than usual maybe."

"Oh, no," she said softly, her face gentle, "I think you're beautiful."

Her words, though innocently meant, made my heart jump. She was suddenly much too close! I scrambled awkwardly to my feet. "Do I get coffee before fish this morning?" I choked, trying to cover my confusion and mask the longing I felt for her.

"Of course you do." She stood and smiled at me. "I'll fix your cup and you can drink it by the stream." Her back to me, she continued, "You're not going to believe these fish! If we can catch some we'll have an honest to goodness feast! How does that sound?"

It sounded great! I hadn't had a full stomach for what seemed like years and the thought of a real meal made my mouth water — that, and no breakfast and only a bowl of greens for supper the night before.

As I followed Merry down the ramp and to the stream I promised myself to be more careful with my feelings. Her expression, in those few moments, had been so strange. I could not interpret what I had seen in her eyes. Thank goodness I had not reached for her!

We walked south from our cave for about a hundred yards to a kind of backwater formed by huge rocks lumped near the center of the stream. We sat quietly, me drinking weak, tepid coffee and Merry peering into the deepest water, willing the fish to be there.

They were! Long, thin and silvery, they hung in the water, tails hardly moving, unconcerned by our presence. Merry looked at me over her shoulder. "See," she whispered, "what did I tell you?"

My interest now fully aroused at the sight of so much food, I whispered back confidently, "Merry, I can taste them already!"

"How're we going to catch them? We don't have hooks or whatever."

"No, but we have a sheet and the cords from around our bedrolls. You wait here and I'll go get the stuff to make a net! If the fish leave, follow them, okay?"

"You're kidding, I know, but I'm not going to let them out of my sight. You just hurry back!"

It took only a few minutes to snatch a sheet from my bedroll and grab the cords. Merry was still watching the fish, which hadn't moved. We tied cord to the corners of the sheet and several baseball-size rocks along one bottom edge, then we sneaked the sheet into the water on the far side of the rocks and slowly pulled it around to block the opening so the fish had nowhere to go.

Then we simply dragged the sheet onto the bank. We counted eleven fish flopping frantically.

"Chris, you're a genius!" Ecstatic, she squeezed my arm. "Now who's the girl scout?"

Very pleased at our success, we hurried back to our front yard. I dumped the fish on the ground near the stream and guarded them while Merry went for the knives and the sharpening stone. In a few minutes working together we had them scaled and gutted and ready for the pan.

"I'm going to save the insides, Merry. I think they'll make bait so we can catch other things." I had no idea what other things were available to catch but I was going to try.

Merry carried the fish inside and I helped her build the fire. We put them in the frying pan, then sat and sniffed and watched as they cooked. Then we gorged on plain, more-or-less fried fish, right out of the pan and more delicious than I could ever remember food tasting.

It was a marvelous breakfast, or lunch, and we smiled happily at each other as we licked our fingers clean, a stack of fish bones on the ground between us.

"How would you feel about a good strong cup of coffee right this minute, Chris?"

"I'd love it but isn't it almost gone?"

"Yes, but there's enough for a couple of cups. I'm talking about thick, black coffee."

"You mean shoot the works, don't you?" I knew we could probably stretch what was left, like we had been doing, but it was so weak and tasteless. "Well, let's do it, Merry!"

"I knew you'd agree." Smiling, she put the pot on the fire and we watched it heat. Then, very carefully, she divided the remaining coffee into our two cups and poured the water. Instantly I smelled the wonderful, familiar aroma of our last cup for who knew how long.

We sat on the floor, sipping and enjoying. When the final drop was drained I felt better than I had for the entire week just passed. Merry seemed just as content, I thought.

"Chris," she said almost dreamily, "do you think you could make some kind of chairs so we wouldn't have to sit on the floor? If you're up to it, that is."

Chairs? Chairs? I stared at her. A picture of our two lovely folding chairs flashed into my mind . . . the chairs, the tarp, the stove, the ice chest . . . all left for the storm to claim. "Ah, well, yes I guess . . . I think so."

"And another thing." I waited. "I have to cook squatting on the ground, you know, and it's darned uncomfortable. It'd be okay if we were just camping out for a day or two but . . ."

I thought about it for a second, then I asked her, "If you could have whatever you wanted for a stove, what would it look like?"

She had her answer ready. "It'd be the same height as a regular stove so I could cook standing up. And there'd be a grill on the top and a place for the fire under that and then some way to get rid of the ashes. Maybe a grate that the ashes could fall through." She was looking at me but I knew she was seeing a stove so I didn't say anything.

"Better than that," she started again, "what about a thing to catch the ashes, like a scoop or something, so all I'd have to do is pull it out, empty it, then put it back. That way I wouldn't have to be scraping ashes all the time." She was still looking at me but in her mind I had turned from a stove into a stove maker.

Not wanting to disappoint her or look any less to her, I nodded and said that I'd get started on a stove right away. Or should I make the chairs first?

"The stove, I think. And Chris . . . ."

"Yes?"

"Could you manage a table to go with the chairs?"

* * * * *

It had not occurred to either of us that the stream, so shallow and fast, could have contained fish. Now, however, we knew we could probably manage to have a meal of them when we wanted to and we knew where and how to catch them. We were no longer helpless.

In spite of the availability of fish, most of our time was still taken in a search for food. We both came to realize that there was a very good reason why technology had taken so long to flower. People had to get food. When your every waking hour is spent searching for something to eat, you are simply not in the mood to invent anything.

With Merry's help and advice on the design, over the next week I built the stove she wanted. The bottom part was made of rocks, shaped brick-like with the VW tire tool and the flat part of the hatchet. These we stacked in a "U," about thirty inches high and held together with clay which we found in abundance near the stream. While the clay dried we hacked a square of metal from the bottom of the car, poked it full of holes with the tire tool so ashes would fall through and then sat it on the "U." Then we built the walls another eight or ten inches higher and set our cooking grill, made of the same metal only with fewer holes, on top of that.

Of course, the wood for our stove had to be hand cut, not more than sixteen inches long or it wouldn't fit, but that wasn't a problem as we saw it. We had plenty of time to chop wood. I spent three whole days just cutting limbs to the right length and chopping away side branches so Merry would have a pile of dry wood about four feet tall as a back-up. "When the stack gets low," I told her, "I'll chop more."

Then, to show my expertise, my first wood-working project was going to be a rocking chair. From a grove of evergreen trees growing south of us by the stream I cut slender, supple branches to use as the chair's support, the basic shape. There were vines aplenty climbing our cliff — thick, sturdy, easily reached; and in an hour I hacked enough to wrap the joints of several chairs. My plan was to make each of us a comfortable rocker. I started working about noon and kept at it through the afternoon, working and reworking the design because I had forgotten which part to do when. Finally, at dusk, not yet finished, I tested and discovered that my chair was more inclined to collapse than rock. Defeated, I abandoned that particular design and began turning it into a straight-leg chair instead. Many frustrating hours of labor the next day produced what looked like a wooden cage on stilts and was as comfortable as a device of medieval torture. Bent wood furniture, I found, was not hard to make if you didn't intend to use it. The hard part was getting it to hold together without nails or staples. I tried to wind vine around the critical parts but if the vine was thick it wouldn't wind and the thinner vines cracked and wouldn't hold.

"Tires have wire in them, Chris," Merry informed me. So we burned a tire on the cliff top and found miles and miles of wire that could be used in making furniture and other things as well.

Now that I had the wire, I was ready to start building furniture that we could actually use. So I gathered my supplies and started to work on a small sofa.

After I had worked for a while I heard, "Chris, why don't you make a couple of stools first so we can have something to sit on and then work on more elaborate designs once we're sitting?" Merry was trying to hide a smile. "I'm sure you can do them perfectly once you're not so rushed."

I looked at her from where I was sitting in a tangle of wire and pieces of wood and gnarled vines. Her eyes were brimming tears from trying to hold back the laughter. I thought it was funny, too, but was too exasperated to let my own laughter surface.

"Well, damn it, Merry, I just forgot how to put these things together. I used to know." And I scowled at the mess around me. I heard Merry choking, and darted a frowning glance at her. She was bent over, shaking with laughter. I couldn't hold it in any longer. I began to laugh, too. We both howled until we were weak.

Merry, sniffing and wiping her face on her shirt sleeve, came and sat beside me on the log. She put her arm around my waist and leaned her head on my shoulder. "You know I wasn't laughing at you, don't you? It's just that things have been so grim and your sofa looked so funny! It felt good to laugh for a change."

I was so conscious of Merry's softness and warmth that I felt myself shiver from wanting her. "Well," I said grudgingly, "I found it kind of funny, too." I turned my head and looked at her so close to me, our legs touching, her body snug against me. It took all my strength, but I stood. "I'll clean up this mess in the morning, Merry. Will that be all right?" She seemed so tiny and forlorn, sitting there.

"Sure, I'll even help." There was something in her eyes, an expression I couldn't read this time, either.

One day, I thought, you're going to touch me like that and I'm going to touch you back, little lady, promise or no promise. And on that thought, I went to bed.

Chapter VIII

Those first weeks, almost constantly hungry, our hunger sharpened by our physical exertions, we cooked and ate whatever we could find. We dug for crawling things in the stream bed and sat for hours at what we thought was a game trail, waiting for something edible to appear.

We did find berries, several kinds, but too green to eat. They did have the possibility of being food when they ripened. We also found tiny, shriveled fruit-like things on the ground that we ate only as a last resort but they helped us survive to look for more.

We gathered eggs from the nests we could reach on the cliff face and we ate them in every form we could think of. It took dozens of the tiny things to make a meal but we had hundreds within easy reach. I was afraid at first that we'd scare the birds away but they always came back.

* * * * *

Merry was looking at the iridescent black birds that swooped and soared over our cliff. I had tried throwing rocks at them but succeeded only in making my arm sore. I looked up at the birds, too. All that food so near but yet so far!

"Chris, have you ever used a slingshot?"

"Can't say that I ever have."

"I'll bet you could hit them if you had something to aim, like a slingshot, and if you could hit them we could have a blackbird pie!"

I sighed. "We need a rubber band to make a slingshot."

"I think we have rubber. I think we have enough to make several slingshots, as a matter of fact."

"We do?" I didn't remember seeing rubber bands in our pitiful supplies.

"Think about inner tubes in tires, Chris. They're made of rubber, aren't they? And didn't we take a tube out of the tire we burned?"

Yes, we did have an inner tube and soon we had a slingshot. We had several of them, in fact, made of different shapes and different kinds of wood. We collected and stacked a pile of small stones at the bottom of the cliff and then we set out to collect our supper. If we had not been so serious and so hungry our efforts would have been funny. We hit everything but the birds at first; then we began to come close, then closer, and soon we had fourteen birds on the ground at the foot of the cliff. This was due not to our skill but to the fact that there were so many birds congregated in one place. If we didn't hit the one we aimed at we hit the one next to it.

"I think we have enough for the pot, don't you?" Merry was jubilant.

We carried our collection of birds to the stream and placed them carefully on the ground, then we looked at each other. I was the first to speak. "Merry, have you ever cleaned a bird?"

"Um, yes, chickens. But they didn't have feathers and the insides were wrapped in paper. I don't think that counts, do you?"

We looked at each other over the pile of feathers and beaks and feet. Even the eyes were still open.

"In my whole life," I said, "I never thought I'd kill a bird. I never thought I'd want to eat a bird, either. But Merry, I'm so hungry that I'm ready to eat feathers and all." I looked at the birds again. "Tell you what." I knelt and picked up a tiny body. "I'm going to cut off the heads and you pull off the feathers. Then I'll cut them open and take out the insides and you wash them, okay?"

Merry was nodding, not very enthusiastically, but she took the decapitated body I handed her and began plucking feathers.

We ate roasted birds and greens that very afternoon. The birds only made about two mouthfuls each but we didn't care.

It was a start.

* * * * *

What had, at first, been hazy speculation about our whereabouts became a frightening reality one rainy afternoon at the end of March. We were indoors because of the weather. Greens were bubbling in our tiny pot and six slender fish were baking, more or less, in the frying pan. Merry was sitting on one of our new bent-wood stools with her back to our door and was using what little light there was to leaf through the fossil book.

"I don't believe this!" I heard her say. "Chris, come look, hurry!"

I had been stripping the bark from willow-like limbs, trying to remember how to make a three-legged table by bending or braiding the supple wood into the proper shape. Mostly, I was exasperated because what I had made did not look like a table or anything resembling furniture as we know it. I was glad to quit.

I knelt next to Merry and she held the book out to me. "Look at this!"

I saw a dinosaur chewing on the top limbs of a tree. "Yes, what?"

"The trees, look at the trees!"

I looked at the trees on the page. They were shorter than the animals, they had brown trunks and green foliage. They were just trees. I started to say this to Merry but then my brain caught up with my eyes. My mouth probably dropped open but no words came out.

"See, they're the same ones, aren't they?"

I was still staring at the page.

"Aren't they?" Merry jiggled my arm impatiently.

I nodded. "Do you know what this means?"

"I think I do but I wish I didn't. Trees like that haven't existed for millions of years but we have them growing all over the place. Not only the trees —" Her eyes were huge. "— but think of those weird plants and shrubs we couldn't find in the foraging book, I'll bet they're going to be in this one!"

She began flipping pages and we both scrutinized the foliage painted in as background for pictures of long extinct animals.

"I've seen this!" She pointed to a page. "And this, too!" She pointed to another page.

"Yeah, and these are growing all over the place." I put my finger on a drawing of cycadeoid plants being eyed by an eighty-seven foot Diplodocus. All of this taking place in the Jurassic period which began a hundred and eighty million years ago, according to the fossil book, and ended a hundred and thirty-five million years ago.

Merry shivered. "If the foliage is here wouldn't that animal be here, too?"

"I don't know. But, uh, if the foliage is here then we can't be here, right? I mean, people didn't exist when this animal was alive on earth but we're people and we're here so if we're here maybe the animals aren't." I knew what I was saying didn't make sense but Merry was nodding charitably as if it did.

For the moment our conversation was brought to a halt by the odor of burning fish. "Damn!" Merry groaned. "That's our supper on fire!" And we both dove to the rescue, visions of reptilian tooth and tail momentarily forgotten.

* * * * *

I had eaten three singed fish. Merry was still stirring her fish around on the plate.

"Chris, I've been thinking and I'm really beginning to get scared. There's no earthly reason for this place to have trees extinct for millions of years. Extinct things don't live next to modern things." She was shaking her head. "Anyway, if they're extinct, that means they aren't around any more, doesn't it? What kind of place is this, anyway?"

"I wish I knew, Merry. I have an idea, though. You'll probably say it's crazy but maybe . . ."

I cleared my throat and wiped my mouth on my sleeve. "It's the lightning, you see. It somehow picked us up and sent us here, or brought us here or whatever, and it does the same thing to plants and stuff. Probably a hundred and eighty million years ago it picked up those trees and the shrubs and they got planted here, same as the other trees and things that we recognize."

"Okay, I'll buy that, but you haven't carried the thought far enough." She was very serious. "If those things have been here for a hundred and eighty million years they'd have evolved into whatever they eventually became or they'd have become extinct again and not be here at all. Right?"

I had to think about that for a minute. I took in a deep breath and started again. "Well, think about this. What if the extinct things belong here and all of the other things, us included, have just arrived. Compliments of the lightning, of course."

"You mean this is a prehistoric valley and we're the new people on the block? Us and some of the trees and some of the fish and birds and turtles or whatever there is around here that's familiar to us? Let me give you more food for thought. Suppose this is an ordinary valley, okay? Except that it's the valley that was here a hundred and eighty million years before our time, before erosion wore it down to the flat place where we went camping a few weeks ago. Now, we both think that the lightning is the local means of transportation, right?" She wasn't looking at me but was staring into the dying fire. "And if we can accept that as fact, we shouldn't have any problem believing that the lightning moved us in time but not in space." She shook her head slowly. "And that this valley was here, just as it is now, at the same time that we were living where we were. In other words, everything that ever was, still is!"

Her last sentence flattened itself against my mind then slid to the floor. I chose to ignore it. Instead, I said, "You mean we're in the same place where we were that Friday night but the time is one hundred and eighty million years ago?" I could feel the hair on the back of my neck bristle. "That means we're not only the oldest people on earth but the only people on earth, doesn't it?"

Merry nodded slowly. "And we're likely to get older than that waiting for someone to find us. They're looking for us a hundred and eighty million years too late."

This sobered me utterly. "Well, however we got here and wherever we are, I'm just glad those dinosaurs aren't around. I don't think my slingshot would be any kind of a match for them."

Merry, her eyes still on the glowing coals, did not answer.

* * * * *

I had wanted to be alone with Merry but not to the extent that we actually were . . . not as the only two people on earth. Whether we were on some other plane but co-existing with the world we knew, or had been carried back to an earth many millions of years younger than the one we left, was unimportant in our day-to-day existence. We were physically here and all our efforts were expended in keeping ourselves alive in the here and now. I thought often of my office, of Sylvia and Bessie. I had not been as family or socially oriented as Merry and I yearned more for creature comforts than for people. It was different with Merry. Both of her parents were living and she worried that the shock of her disappearance would further wound her father's ailing heart.

We were both awed by the silence of our valley and welcomed the early morning commotion of the birds sharing our cliff. Perhaps we talked more than was absolutely necessary but we found comfort in the sound of each other's voice, no matter the words.

I was still finding it very hard to get through a day without cigarettes. Merry missed the morning paper and that first eye-opening cup of coffee. After some discussion we decided that wishing for the things we missed only made it harder to enjoy the few comforts we actually had. Our cave was snug, we had a variety of food, clean water, wood for cooking and heat and we were both in good health. "I won't if you won't," Merry said bravely. "No more wishing for things, okay?"

I nodded and smiled. She had no idea what I longed for most.

* * * * *

So far we had seen no large animals. There were signs of smaller ones, however, and I set out to hunt them. Any aversion I may have had about killing was far in my past, not likely to surface as long as I wanted food for Merry and me.

Knowing about primitive hand weapons kept us alive and eating. I made a larger, very powerful slingshot and after much practice could hit anything that came within range. At first we were squeamish about skinning the small creatures and birds that I managed to hit but soon we could strip off fur or feathers and clean body cavities without giving it a thought.

I used animal parts and entrails, fish heads and fish guts as bait in the live traps I fashioned from slender branches and vines that were easy to form into the shape I thought a trap should have. Since we were trying to catch small animals, I made a sort of rectangle about eighteen inches wide and high and twenty-five inches deep. I wove the vines in a criss-cross pattern, making the weave one or two inches apart and leaving one end of the box open as an entrance. Then I added a funnel of small sticks. The mouth of the funnel was large at the open end of the box but became smaller as it entered the trap. I baited the closed end so that the animal had to enter the trap completely in order to eat. Once in, the animal couldn't make its way back through the small end of the funnel. Tire wire held this apparatus rigidly in place.

I became rather proud of my hunting abilities. Soon I had a line of traps on both sides of the stream and usually caught two or three small furry things each time I checked.

The animals I killed were all very lean so we had little fat in our diet. Occasionally I would catch a turtle and then we would delight in turtle stew. Merry cooked the chunks of meat with a potato-like root, diced into small pieces and flavored with green onion tops we'd found along the stream bed. Maybe they weren't actually onions but they tasted like onions and smelled like onions and we enjoyed them wholeheartedly. We found other tasty, tender greens growing on the bank and in the shallows, and a tubular shoot from a sort of water lily proved to be very sweet and filling.

Eventually Merry dried the tiny, new leaves from a reddish plant that grew in border-like profusion along the root system of certain trees and made our tea. The taste was slightly tart but the color was the same as tea and soon we couldn't remember tea tasting any other way. I did prefer sweetener but unsweet tea was better than no tea, I found.

There were plants that provided us with mint, lemon and liquorice flavors for sipping in our tea or flavoring a side dish. The lemon-smelling leaves Merry also crushed and strained in the water when we washed our hair.

There wasn't a leaf or a vine or a root in our area that we didn't try to eat or make use of in one form or another. Some things had no taste and others had too much but there was a great variety of textures and flavors and we boiled and stewed and dried and roasted whatever we thought would add to our diet.

Merry's book on wild edibles probably saved us from poison more than once. We examined every plant, bush and tree, using the guide to help us identify whatever it was that we wanted to put in the pot. If the whatever even faintly resembled something poisonous we didn't eat or touch.

Now that we weren't hungry all the time I made brooms so that we could sweep our house and, at Merry's urging and after much experimentation, finally constructed a wooden table. Then two chairs that were actually comfortable. In time I also made glass-topped tables, large and small, using the windows from the VW.

The car proved to be our salvation. As time passed we thought of a use for almost every part of the little station wagon. Not having a wrench was a handicap I could not always overcome, but for the most part we managed to unscrew, unbolt, break off or tear apart almost everything but the motor and the frame itself.

After that disastrous Friday night, the car stayed tipped over in the gully until we had stripped what we could from the exposed bottom and side. Then we used long poles to turn it right side up so that we could strip the rest of it.

It took me hours to work loose the bolts that held the seats and many more hours taking parts from the engine for possible future use. I made a basket for what we salvaged and we kept every piece, even those we couldn't identify. We saved the oil that hadn't spilled and we found a gallon or so of gas still in the tank, a treasure.

One morning a few weeks later, when it seemed colder than usual, I knew it was time to talk with Merry about something that had been worrying me. As we sat sipping tea after breakfast, I asked if she had given any thought to winter even though we felt it was still months away.

Serious, she nodded. "I wondered when it would occur to you. I hated to mention it because you're working so hard now, but we'll starve if we can't begin to store food somehow."

Almost two months had passed and neither of us mentioned the possibility of being rescued before winter; we somehow didn't talk much about rescue at all these days. Wherever we were, we were cut off completely from civilization as we knew it. To find us, our rescuers would have to know how we got here so they could get here too. And neither Merry nor I knew how the lightning had transferred us to this time, if that was the correct explanation. Or how it had moved us to this place, if that was, indeed, what it had done. I tried not to think about it too much.

Chapter IX

I seldom gave thought to anything anymore. Eight weeks had passed in exhausting activity. Each day there was food to look for, some part of the car to unbolt to use as part of something else, wood to collect, and dozens of small things to do or to make in order to be more comfortable in our cave.

I kept busy from dawn to dark. Often I would be away for an entire day, searching, exploring, hunting. I knew about an atlatl, the throwing spear of ancient peoples, and the missile weapon called a bola which consists of stones attached to the end of thongs which, when twirled and thrown, were supposed to wrap around the prey. I also made a bow of wood which had good spring to it but the bow string would not remain taut and my arrows flew, at most, ten feet in a wavering arc. I tried to use all of these weapons but with little success.

Being bone tired at the end of each day made the nights almost bearable. Merry and I had developed a closeness that should have been satisfying but it only made me ache. I wanted her physically. Many times I had been on the verge of telling her how I felt, how much I needed her, but stopped for fear of her reaction. I was so afraid she would turn from me in disgust. There was only friendship in her manner, nothing more. It was almost painful for me to be with her. Yet she seemed content with our relationship. We smiled good morning and yawned goodnight to each other and this seemed enough for her. It wasn't enough for me, however, and I didn't know how much longer I could disguise my feelings.

Our chores kept us apart most of the day. I hunted and fished and trapped and collected wood. Merry cooked, fished, gathered growing things, kept us and the cave clean, and collected wood.

I had made a fish hook from heavy steel wire out of the VW door. Using chunks of fish as bait, I would go an easy fifteen-minute walk upstream to a place where the water was very deep. There I'd catch a large ferocious-looking fish that had delicious sweet red meat. It had an entirely different flavor from the small white fish we caught near the cliff and except for the spine, was almost boneless.

One afternoon I was sitting on the bank, my line not even in the water, thinking about Merry. Perhaps it was that time of the month but I was feeling especially low. The sound of rushing water covered Merry's footsteps and I didn't know she was there until she touched my shoulder. Startled, I looked up. She knelt with her face close to mine; her concern was evident.

"Chris, what's wrong, is something the matter? Are you all right?"

"Nothing's wrong, Merry, I was just sitting . . . thinking."
Had I said this to her before?

"What were you thinking, hon?"

I was so miserable that her small endearment couldn't cheer me. "I wasn't really thinking anything. I'm okay." I forced a smile.

"Well, I want you to come back with me. I have a surprise!"

We walked together back to the cliff, both of us silent. I just didn't have the heart to make small talk. Merry herself was often silent these days.

As we neared the cliff, I heard birds squalling. Soon I saw the reason for the noise. Merry had somehow caught three turkeys, or what looked like turkeys, and had them each tied by a leg to a small tree.

"I thought I'd start our flock," she told me proudly.

Who's to say what makes our feelings run high one minute and low the next? All I know is that the sight of Merry standing expectantly, hands on her hips, waiting for some kind of reaction from me, caused such a feeling of depression that I found it hard to breathe.

I tried, I really tried, but all I could manage was, "That's great, Merry. Shall I build a pen?" And I turned and walked away. I had to, I was about to cry.

"Wait, Chris!"

I stopped and turned. For a long minute we looked at each other. Then Merry, dropping her gaze, turned away from me.

What had I communicated in those seconds? Had she seen my misery? Found desire written all over my face? If so, it had not made any difference to her. I walked on.

At a shallow bend in the stream there were slender young trees growing. I began cutting them with my hatchet, to make a pen of sorts for the birds. I chopped viciously, hacking furiously at the wood as if to release on it some of the hurt and anger and frustration I felt. With this kind of chopping I accomplished more in an hour than I ordinarily would have in two.

In spite of this, it was growing dark before I had cut what I thought was enough wood. Collecting my hatchet and as many of the poles as I could carry, I walked along the stream towards our cave. I walked slowly, not feeling the weight of the wood on my shoulder, not really noticing the early chill in the air.

I had to go to the cave, there was no place else to go, but I would rather have bedded down on the stream bank, cold or not. My heart was a leaden lump in my chest.

Even before I entered, I could smell stew simmering on our stove. I dropped a couple of short pieces of wood in the wood bin, washed my hands in the fender well we used as a sink and sat at the table. Neither of us had spoken.

Merry served my portion then filled her bowl and we ate silently. My mouth was so dry I almost choked on every bite.

"It's good, Merry," I finally told her.

She smiled her thank you.

I pushed back from the table and with an exaggerated yawn I said, "Think I'll turn in early, I'm kind of tired." Expecting no answer from her and hearing none, I heated water, sponged myself clean and slipped into my sleeping bag, turning my back to her and the room.

All this time she had sat silently staring into the fire. I heard her cleaning our dishes and the tiny noises she made as she, too, bathed in warm water. The fire was low now and I listened for the sound of her zipping her sleeping bag.

The sound did not come. Instead, I felt her hand on my shoulder.

She did not speak and I waited. Finally, I turned on my back and looked at her. I could not see her expression, she was a silhouette against the fire's embers.

But I heard her breath catch, then her voice low and hesitant. "Chris, I . . . I'm in love with you. Please," she begged, "let me come in with you tonight."

I could not believe my ears. Without speaking, because I couldn't, I drew my arms out from the bag and touched her face. My fingers felt the wetness of tears on her cheeks.

I heard her sob. When she touched my face lightly with her fingertips, she felt tears on my face also.

With my help she moved into the bag with me and we lay, naked, our bodies touching but neither of us moving.

She started slowly, "I've never let myself believe it could be like this but I've loved you and I've wanted to . . . sleep . . . with you almost from the first. I thought if we were together you could learn to feel the same for me but I've seen that it's not that way with you . . . You always move away when I get near . . . or when I touch you . . . but if you'll let me stay I'll do anything you like . . . please, Chris, please don't be angry . . ."

To hush her, I covered her lips with mine.

I felt her arms around my shoulders, pulling me to her. "Oh, Chris," she whispered, "Oh my love . . ."

Those first kisses were tentative, hesitant, as if we were both afraid to prolong the contact. But suddenly, in a single instant for both of us, the barricades fell and we joined mouths in a meeting that left us shaking with desire.

"I love you, too," I breathed into her ear.

"I love you, too," I said to her eyes, her mouth, her lovely breasts that I had wanted to taste for so long.

"I have always loved you," I said as my fingers, wet with her lubricant, slipped inside her.

"Always and always and always," began the litany of our love.

Soon she was thrusting against my hand and I could not keep up with her. I put my leg between hers to hold my hand in place as she moved faster. Then her body stilled for a long moment.

In the time it took for her breathing to slow I covered her face with kisses. "I love you, I love you," I told her. "From the moment I first saw you I have loved you with all my heart." I held her close, feeling the rapid beat of her heart, the warmth and softness of her pressed against me.

She moved in the circle of my arms, turning so that our faces were touching, our legs intertwined. Our lips touched and I took her tongue in my mouth, felt the pressure of her thigh between my legs, her hand on my breast. I gasped as her fingers found the nipple, then moved down my body to touch, to dip into, the wetness flowing from me.

She sat up. "I love you the most," she said, kneeling to open my legs. Then she lowered her face.

The touch of her tongue was light and dainty, just a teasing flicker, followed by the faintest breath as she blew softly on those places where her tongue had been.

Her hands found my breasts and she teased the nipples with her fingers, matching the movement of her tongue.

I tried to exert some control to make it easy for her to love me but she wanted to make long, slow love. Her tongue exploring then dipping into me with tidy little movements. Celibacy for so long had left me with a desperate need but as the night passed I could often hold back for a while allowing her to spend longer and longer at her task.

My joy was total and complete. It was, I know, the happiest night of my life.

* * * * *

I think we awoke at the same instant. Sometime in the night we had zipped the sleeping bags together and were sleeping back to back. We both turned to reach for the other. I needed to know that the night had not been a dream; she needed the reassurance also. And so, for a long moment, we held each other tightly.

"I love you," she whispered.

"I love you," I whispered back.

We washed together, kissed many times, held hands as we drank our tea.

I stood behind her, arms circling her waist as she scrambled eggs for our breakfast.

I kissed her as she served our plates, the kiss becoming longer and longer as we clung together.

The feel of her soft breasts pressing into me started that delicious throb between my legs, her tongue on mine added to the growing desire I felt for her.

Her hand moved down and touched me lightly. My jeans were suddenly a barrier.

She opened the snap, lowered the zipper and touched my bare skin.

Breakfast forgotten, we moved back to our bed. How pleased I was to find that she wanted me as much as I wanted her.

* * * * *

The turkeys proved to be more of a problem than we both wanted.

"Merry, darling," — I could call her that now — "if we pen these things then we'll have to feed them."

"Oh?" She had not thought of that. "I wanted them so we would have a sort of walking dinner, like available at any time," she informed me. "If we can have animals we can kill when we want them and not have to hunt . . ." She trailed off.

"You mean like on a real farm, don't you?"'

She nodded and stared at the turkeys still tied to the tree but quieter now.

"That's wonderful, my love." I had to keep saying it, it sounded so good to me. "But we don't have waving fields of grain to feed them and they probably eat plenty!"

The birds' tiny eyes stared at us and we stared at them.

"I thought you'd be so happy. You know I want to make you happy, don't you?" She put her arm around my waist and leaned her beautiful head on me.

I kissed that bright hair while the birds watched us unblinkingly. "Tell you what. I'll clip their wings so they can't fly away and we'll keep them tied to the tree for a day or two and feed them what we can and maybe when we let them loose they'll stick around."

Merry was loathe to let a possible meal walk away but agreed to let me try.

Clipping the wings was not easy. I didn't have clippers in the first place and didn't know which part of the wing to clip with the clippers I didn't have. I was only thankful that feathers didn't have feelings. It was one thing to kill cleanly but hacking away at the wings made me feel like a monster. There was a lot of squawking and flapping, but finally I had more feathers on the ground than the birds had on their now nearly naked wings.

We gave them fresh water in one of our pots and huge handfuls of the green leaf that we found so tasty. I emptied some berries on the ground and threw them some of the shriveled orange-colored fruits that were not so tasty. The birds fell to and scratched and gobbled and ate with much enthusiasm. They were not happy to be tied to the tree but the availability of so much food seemed to make up for their imprisonment.

Merry said I was a genius for thinking of clipping their wings. I told her she was smarter than that for catching them in the first place.

"I really didn't catch them, my darling." She had to keep saying things like that, too. "They just appeared. The big one walked up to me and went gobble, gobble and shook his feathers while the other two just stood there. So I got the cord and made a big noose and put a fish head on the ground in the middle and here we are, a turkey farm!"

I had to kiss her again for being even smarter than I thought. We hugged there in the open, under the broad blue sky, the turkeys watching but keeping their thoughts to themselves.

After a while we decided that all three turkeys were from our own time, mostly tame and accustomed to being fed by people. They were, we felt, waifs of the lightning, too.

Chapter X

I was down by the stream cleaning the meat of a small animal I had caught in one of my traps. We were now in our fourth month in this place. The water was loud as it rushed over the rocky stream bed and fell into the depression we had dug for washing clothes and cleaning food, so I wasn't sure at first just what it was I heard or if I had actually heard anything. I sat back on my heels and listened for a long minute, trying to hear over the water.

"Merry," I said when I returned to our cave, "I heard the funniest noise just now down by the stream. It sounded like a child crying." At her look, I grinned and added, "Maybe it was a baby bird. Or maybe I imagined it."

She caressed my cheek, her touch soft, loving. "You do have a lively imagination. I can say that for you."

Her smile told me she was remembering the previous night. I can say one thing about our lovemaking, we were both totally unselfconscious and would try, enthusiastically, any suggestion the other made.

Merry was carrying her largest bowl, the one with a handle of braided plastic stitching from the VW seats strung through holes on three sides. "I saw some huge greens growing in the bend of the stream yesterday and I want to pick some for supper. Want to come with me?"

I thought for a moment. "No, I'd better finish here. I want to clean my hands and get some firewood and haul some bath water . . ."

Merry stopped me. "Wash your hands and come with me and I'll help you with the wood and the water, okay?"

Always happier when we were together, I put the meat on our glass-topped kitchen counter and we walked together down the ramp to the stream. I squatted and washed my hands, then we followed the bank upstream till we reached the bend.

Merry began picking the bright green leaves, rinsing them in the clear running water. She was wearing shorts and a sleeveless shirt, and her golden hair was gathered and tied with a piece of cloth. Her movements were beautiful to watch. There is not one thing awkward about her and as I looked I could see her as she was last night, naked, her body moving under mine, eyes half closed . . .

Aware of me watching, she straightened and grinned, her teeth white and perfect. She had read my thoughts.

"Do you have something else in mind, Chris darling, or are you going to look for wood?"

"Actually, I was going to look for wood," I answered, "but maybe something else would be more appropriate to the way I'm feeling."

"Whatever you're feeling will have to wait until I finish gathering these leaves and get them home and in the pot. You do want dinner, don't you?"

I was about to tell her that we could have both when I heard the sound again. Merry heard it, too, for she stiffened and looked around, her eyes wide. It was the same sound I'd heard earlier, like a child sniffing and crying.

I thought it was coming from the other side of the stream and without thinking I jumped into the water and crashed my way to the opposite bank. Lucky for me the stream at that spot wasn't much over knee-deep. My tennis shoes were almost falling apart but the rubber soles kept me from killing my feet on the rocky bottom.

I stopped on the bank and listened again. No more sobbing, but I did hear something in the high weeds almost at my feet. Heart pounding, I began thrashing away, tearing at the brush, bound to find whatever it was.

"Chris, be careful!" Merry was behind me.

"It's right here, Merry . . ." I began. Then I stopped. I heard Merry gasp then we both fell to our knees beside the ragged bundle that lay on the ground.

It was a little boy. What clothing he wore was in tatters, there was blood dried in a hundred scratches, and bone showed through several deep cuts on his legs, the wounds ugly and oozing. He had covered his eyes with his hands, his thin chest convulsed as he drew each breath. He moaned as Merry picked him up and cradled him in her arms. His head, scabrous and filthy, fell on her shoulder.

The greens and the wood forgotten, we ran back to our cave.

Merry knew what to do. "Get more water and heat it, Chris, and hand me that shirt of yours . . . dampen it first in that warm water on the stove and then put a little weak meat broth in a cup for him to drink."

She bathed the poor thin body, tenderly patting away the dirt and dried blood, examining each gouge and welt and suppurating wound. His eyes, partially open and leaking fluid, followed her face. His crying had stopped. His breathing was almost regular and he didn't wince as the painful procedure continued.

He would not, or could not, drink the broth. Merry poured small amounts into his mouth but it wouldn't go down. She rubbed his throat the way you would to make an animal swallow but still the fluid ran out.

Merry was crooning to him as she gently went over the poor, wasted body with the damp cloth. In spite of the pain she must have caused he seemed to understand that she was trying to help him. He did not smile but his face relaxed.

Finally, Merry was finished. There was little she could do about the wounds. Two of them were surely gangrenous, the flesh black in places and with yellow, bloody pus leaking at the edges.

He was probably six years old. When I first saw him, lying dirty there on the ground, I thought he might have been the child of a cave family or of nomads. But the rags that hung on him were secured by buttons and there was a scrap of plastic zipper attached to the cloth around his waist. We cut away the material with a knife and I examined it closely. I found no labels but there was no strangeness about the fabric or the belt loops or the buttons.

"Merry," I whispered, "he could be one of the missing children we were always hearing about. Remember the pictures all over the place of kids missing or lost?"

She nodded. "How did he get here, Chris?"

"The same way we did, probably."

We put him down on our bed and covered him, his body making only a tiny bump under the cover. Not asleep, eyes still half open, his breathing regular but shallow, he watched Merry's face as she knelt beside him and took one of his hands in hers.

We stayed that way for a long time, neither of us speaking, just waiting.

"I need some tea," Merry said, "and we have to think about what to do." When she rose from beside him, he made a tiny noise and his head turned after her.

"I'll be right back, darling," Merry said to him with a smile, then she turned to me. I put my arms around her and held her and she began to sob. "Chris, he's almost starved to death."

"I know, Merry." That was all I could think of to say.

We had tea, Merry going to him half a dozen times before she finished her cup. "One of us should stay up tonight in case he needs something. Maybe we could get him to drink the broth if we keep trying." She was putting off facing what we both could see we had to face and, to my eyes, face very soon.

Late in the night, both of us still awake, she picked him up and held him in her arms. She talked softly to him and he would watch her face but made no response.

Near dawn, the quick little breaths stopped. Merry looked down at the still body in her arms and her tears came, falling on his head as it lay against her.

I took the child from her but then didn't know what to do with him. It was still dark, too dark to dig a grave even if I had a shovel. Leaving him in the room didn't seem to be the right thing, either.

Undecided, I stood there until Merry said, "Let's put him in our hall on some straw and in the morning we'll bury him."

She collected an armful of straw from the foot of our bed and placed it on the ground in the hallway. I laid him down and straightened his limbs and Merry covered him with my shirt. Then we went back inside.

Of course we couldn't go to sleep. We held each other and whispered back and forth until it was light. I told her that he had probably come many weeks ago when there had been a rather fierce lightning storm. "He may not even have been from America," I told her. "He could have been French or Spanish or anything. Remember, he didn't seem to know what you were saying?"

"Oh, Chris, what if we'd found him sooner, he'd be alive now."

I agreed to this but spent the rest of the time trying to convince her that what had happened to him wasn't our fault and that we had done all that we could, that at least he had been held in her warm and loving arms at the end.

When the sun was up, we took him down stream and, with our hands and a makeshift scoop of VW fender, gouged out a hole and put him in it.

He was so tiny that there was hardly a mound when we replaced the gravely sand. Later, at Merry's request, I fashioned a cross from two branches wired together and pounded it into the ground at the head of the grave.

We were both sad because of the child and neither of us could seem to cheer the other. It began to weigh on me, so about a week after it happened I faced Merry with it.

I sat her down beside me on our two-person sofa. She leaned her head on my shoulder and sighed but I made her sit up and look at me.

"Merry, are you all right and in good health? And am I okay and in good health?"

Yes, she nodded.

"And do we love each other and do we have food and shelter?"

Yes, again.

"Are we safe and warm?"

Her head was bobbing, yes, yes, yes!

"Should we let what happened to that poor baby drag us both down into misery so that we can't appreciate the good things we have?"

She shook her head, no.

"Well, sweetheart, could we both try to get on with living? I've been sad, just like you have, but I don't want to be sad for the rest of my life."

She could tell that I meant what I said. For a long minute neither of us spoke. Then Merry leaned forward and kissed me.

"You're right. I think I got into the habit of feeling sad even when I didn't have any need to feel that way. I'm sorry for that baby but being sorry doesn't help him and it certainly doesn't help either of us." She kissed me again.

There are many, many good things I can say in praise of my Merry. She is good-natured, with a smooth, even disposition and a very matter-of-fact, practical way of dealing with things. She was being practical now.

"I'm glad you stopped me, darling, before I slid too far down in the dumps. You are wonderful and I love you!"

We had cleared the air but there was still one more thing.

"Honey, remember the day we found him? You were picking greens and I was watching you? Remember asking me if I had something on my mind?"

Solemnly, she nodded, a tiny smile forming. "I remember," she said.

"Well, that something is still on my mind." We had not made love in over a week and now, with her sitting so close . . .

"Would you like for me to make love to you?" she asked, touching my lips with a finger.

"Please," I answered.

"Put that way, how can I refuse." And her soft lips touched my eyes, my cheeks, my nose and, finally, my mouth. We sat there on our couch, kissing, touching, gradually undressing, touching some more.

We moved to our bed and made love slowly, gently, our passion as high as ever but our expression of it different.

For some days we didn't mention the boy, as if not talking about him would mean he never was. Eventually, we could talk about what happened without the deep sadness.

The little cross, leaning somewhat, still stood over the grave.

Merry's tears had been, I think, caused by the awful condition of his poor, wasted body but her tender heart was actually crying for us.

Chapter XI

"Chris, didn't you tell me that you knew how to make pottery?"

"Ummmm."

"Well, could you teach me?"

We were lying in bed, just awake. It was light but the sun was still behind the mountains and my only thought was to turn over and nap for a few more minutes.

"Chris!" Merry ran a finger tip lightly up my arm, across my shoulder, up my neck and into my ear. "Chris! Calling Chris!"

Sleep impossible now, I opened one eye, grumbling, "Do you have to talk about pottery when we're wrapped around each other and it's dark in here and I haven't had a kiss in hours?"

"Yes I do. And you have so had a kiss. You had plenty of them if I remember correctly. You had plenty of everything else, too." She threw back the cover and sat up, looking down at me. "I want to make some dishes and things and I want you to get up and show me how."

"Now? You want me to get up now? It's not even dawn yet!"

"But I'm wide awake and so you might as well get up." She picked up the cover and wrapped it Indian fashion around her shoulders as she walked to the kitchen end of our room. I heard wood clattering and, after a moment, the sound of Merry fanning the live coals with the reed fan I had made for her. It was chilly there on the floor so I rolled myself in the bottom sleeping bag that we used as a mattress, pulling it over my head. I closed my eyes again, knowing as I did so that it would avail me not one extra moment of sleep.

I was right. We were outside, dressed and sipping hot tea before the sun was half an inch over the mountain tops.

"Merry," I was saying, "it's not that simple. You don't just flap the clay around a few times and make a dish. It has to be fired — that's supposing that this clay will even bake at all. And first you have to, well, everything has to be done first." She had her lip poked out so I knew there was nothing to do but show her how impossible it was going to be.

The clay I had used in that other time was sold in plastic-wrapped packages, ready for the potter. It only needed inventive fingers to bring out what the imagination saw in it. The clay I had to work with now was still part of the stream bank and, "It needs to be washed and cleaned and wedged to the right consistency, then we'd have to test it to see if it's strong enough. And if it wasn't, we have to add sand or some aggregate to give it stability. And all of this takes time!"

I was out of breath already and I hadn't even told her about adding wood ash to lower the firing temperature or what slip was.

"I know all those things are necessary," Merry said patiently, not at all awed by my inexhaustible store of objections, "but I don't have to learn everything at one time. Just tell me what to do first and I'll do that and then tell me what to do second and I'll see if I can do that, too."

I had finished my tea so I put the cup on the bank next to me then took off my boots. "First," I said to her, "we'll walk across the stream and get some clay."

Merry slipped her feet out of her ragged tennis shoes and stood. Taking my hand in hers she said, Isn't it better to begin with simple things, darling? Now, while we're getting the clay you can explain some of those other things to me so I'll understand what we're doing when the time comes to do it."

This was the kind of beginning that Merry liked and it worked just fine. We spent several days working with the clay, trying different proportions of clay and sand and water until we had a mixture that held up and seemed workable. It took one day to build our first kiln which was mostly an open fire pit. We had to rebuild and redesign it several times over the next weeks but each time we improved on the construction. Our final oven was more like a regular kiln; a stone-lined, covered hole with air vents and a fire pit underneath. It was crude but it worked.

Merry spent many happy afternoons building her pots and plates, impressing them with various decorative designs by using a pointed stick or a piece of wood or stone with an unusual shape. She was always delighted when her pieces fired without slumping or breaking.

I kept the kiln woodpile full so Merry wouldn't have to spend her time hauling. There were so few personal things we could do for each other that I was glad to have this simple activity on my part give her so much pleasure.

She rewarded me by making a special cup. It was decorated with little clay flowers in a ring and in the ring she had inscribed *Merry loves Chris.*

* * * * *

Merry, busy scaling fish, had stopped to wash her hands in the stream. She squatted there for a minute then stood and turned to me. "Chris, the next thing I'd like to do is plant a garden."

I was busy gutting the fish she had scaled. "Plant a garden?" I said. I stared up at her. She was looking at me, all innocence, her eyes wide. This was, I knew, a continuation of our conversation at supper last night. Merry had insisted that we needed a garden and I had agreed except that I didn't think we could plant one at this time of year. "Aren't gardens planted in the early spring? And it's past spring, I think." It was, in fact, the middle of summer even if it seemed too cold to be August.

And that, to me, had been the end of it. I was willing to plant in the spring; would enjoy planting in the spring; planned to plant in the spring.

"I have definitely heard of gardens being planted in the summer and also in autumn." And this had been Merry's last word until now.

I sighed. "I am in favor of planting a garden in the next five minutes, Merry, but I don't have gas for the tractor."

She raised her eyebrows. I waited for them to come down but they didn't. I said, "I don't have a hoe." Then I said, "I don't have any seeds." Next I said, "Where do you want it planted?"

It was her idea to clear a small plot between the stream and the gully and try transplanting some of the green leafy things that were a staple in our diet. She also wanted to move grapevines and berry bushes and try to get them started so we wouldn't have to go so far to collect the fruit.

"Merry, I don't know much about farming but I do know that you can't transplant grapevines this time of year. I think you have to do it when the leaves fall or when they're dormant or when the sap's either up or down or whatever."

"You're probably right but I want to try it anyway."

So we cleared a space and after the earth had been softened by rain we turned it as best we could with our makeshift shovel of VW fender and many hours of back-breaking labor. We buried animal and fish guts as fertilizer and then dug up and replanted some green, leafy things that grew along the water's edge upstream and transplanted some small grapevines that had only a few leaves on them.

In spite of the water we gave them, some of the plants wilted and did not recover. A few other looked sick for a day or two but then took root and began to grow. The grapevines took a long time to decide to live but they finally put out more tiny leaves and then little tendrils and seemed to thrive.

After a couple of weeks it was kind of nice to look out of our door and see a garden. Merry enjoyed it hugely and was always digging up something to bring home, "Just to see if it'll grow, sweetheart."

I made a hoe for her out of a sturdy pole and VW metal, and Merry kept the garden as neat as our cave. She made special jugs for carrying water to the garden but, after several weeks, decided that it would be better to irrigate than to carry.

"If you'll dig a shallow trench from the stream to the garden then I'll have the water nearer. Those plants are going to need plenty of water; more than I want to carry, I think."

So I dug the trench and dammed the garden end. When Merry wanted to water her garden she had only to break the dam with her hoe, let the water run where she wanted it to, then rebuild the dam.

"Now, my darling, we have our work cut out for us."

"We do?" I asked, looking at the blisters that trench-digging had given me.

"Yes! We have to start collecting seeds! But first I have to make some jars with tight lids so we can store our seeds over the winter."

"Merry, if I remember, we have to wait until the plants put out flowers and the flowers die before we can collect seeds."

"Of course we do. I just want to be ready, that's all."

"Right!" I said. Then I hugged my Merry because I loved her so much. My Merry hugged me back.

* * * * *

"When I first saw you, that night at Sylvia's, you had the strangest look on your face," Merry said that night as we were reminiscing. "I actually thought you were the loveliest woman in the room. Bessie had told me that she wanted me to meet the smartest person she knew and her best friend so I don't remember what I expected but you quite took my breath away."

Best friend? I didn't know Bessie had felt that way about me.

"And she told me that you and Sylvia were old friends and, for a while before I knew you better, I thought that meant you and Sylvia had been lovers." Turning to look into my face, she touched me lightly under the chin. "And that, my love, meant you were gay and I promised myself that I wasn't going to get involved with any gays!"

"Did I look gay?" I asked, taking her finger between my teeth.

She took her finger from my mouth and lightly ran it around my lips. "No, you looked very stylish and aloof, if slightly pop-eyed."

"Pop-eyed? That's a terrible thing to say to someone who loves you!" I caught her finger with my teeth again.

"I wonder what Bessie and Sylvia are doing now?" Merry turned her body so that she sat between my legs, her back resting against my chest and her head on my shoulder.

"Probably something like this," I answered, touching her ear with my tongue. Slowly I ran my hands down her arms until I held both of her hands in mine.

"Love me," she said and lifted her arms up and around my head, her back arching, her full breasts straining the thin fabric of her shirt.

This is the way we end most of our discussions. This is our dessert after meals. This is what happens when we touch.

I love it when she straddles me and leans down to tease my lips with her breasts. I am allowed to catch what I can with my mouth but must not use my hands.

She sways over me and I suck greedily when a nipple, hard like a tiny bud, is lowered to my tongue.

I wait, breath rasping, for her to lead the way.

Knees apart, she inches her way up my naked body. I feel her weight, the warm wetness, the crisp hair moving slowly upward, finally reaching my heaving chest.

She lifts her body then and kneels over my face and the feasting can begin.

With my hands, I part the silky hair and my tongue searches for the tiny, sensitive spot in the damp nest. I touch it lightly, moving in tiny jerks, circling slowly, then faster. I am aware of my own wetness and close my legs tightly, ankles locked.

Her hips are moving and I know she is close to her climax.

I enter her again and again, tasting her sweetness.

"Ah, Chris!" Merry is now locked in that instant of stillness before the spasms begin. "Chris! Oh, Chris!" Her body is rigid for those few moments as it explodes with pleasure, then I gather her to me, feeling the thudding of her heart next to mine and conscious of the throbbing between my own legs, the head and the wetness.

Her breathing slows and, my own heart pounding, I wait for her touch.

Chapter XII

Not all of each day was spent in trying to feed ourselves. There was always fresh straw to be gathered as a mattress for our bed and the everlasting, unending piles of wood to be collected for cooking and heat. Merry would come to me saying, she needed a this or a that . . . something I could make from wood or car parts. Perhaps a low table, just the right height for a special vase she had made to decorate our cave, or a stool with a flat bottom that wouldn't sink in the sand when she had to sit by the stream to wash something. But a lot of our time was spent trying things that didn't work.

I knew that flour could be made by crushing the meat of acorns, washing and drying, then crushing it again into a powder. When the acorns started falling, we were so hungry for bread that we collected what seemed like tons of huge, fat ones, carrying them back to our cave.

Then, of course, we had to have a table with a flat stone top for the crushing process. The crushed acorns looked great once the shells were removed, like nutty-yellow grain, but the bitterness had to be leached out before we could begin baking. I tied the meal in a double sheet so that running water could pass through and suspended the sheet over the stream from a stout limb. We left it bobbing in the water for three days, until the yellow faded to white. Then we opened the sheet and left it in a sunny spot so the grain could dry. It only too a little more pounding to make the flour finer.

We started with more acorns than we thought we needed and ended with less flour than we thought we wanted but somewhere along the way we left out a vital part of the process. The flour paste we finally cooked was as unpalatable as sand. Even the turkeys had a hard time with it.

"That was too much effort for no reward," Merry said, spitting hoe-cake.

One of the most important jobs was that of keeping the coals hot and glowing in one or the other of our stoves. My cigarette lighter finally gave out of fluid and we had no matches. Keeping the coals alight was Merry's task and it was not easy. If she left the cave and a fire burning for any length of time, chances were it would burn itself out by the time she returned. This kept her more or less tied to the cave or the immediate area.

We kept our few personal possessions, those we had managed to save, on a shelf by our bed. There was some face makeup and lipstick, a tiny mirror, some loose change, binoculars, my wallet, a couple of combs, toothbrushes, a nail file, a little over a hundred dollars in bills, Merry's wallet, my reading glasses, the field guides and our watches ... neither of which had run since the night of the lightning storm.

One day I returned from making the rounds of my traps and found Merry on the ramp, crouched over a smoldering pile of moss and tiny wood chips.

"What's happening, Merry?"

"I'm making a fire, that's what. Look here!"

So I squatted by her, not letting go of my basket with the three squirming little animals inside, and saw that she was focusing the sun's rays through my glasses and onto the dry wood.

"Now, that's darned clever, hon. What made you think of that?"

She blew softly on the moss, causing tiny flames to appear. "The damn fire went out again and I blew and blew till I thought my brains would fall out before I got it started. I knew you could start it with the string and the stick like you've done before but no kidding, that's too primitive for me. So, all of a sudden, I remembered those glasses you hardly ever wear."

Thinking of the hours I had spent twirling a stick before anything happened, I was as delighted as Merry.

She asked, looking at the basket, "Are they going in the cage?"

"Think so. We don't need them right away, do we?" It was now our practice to cage a few of the smaller animals and keep them until needed for a meal. We fed them the same way as the turkeys, or threw them some fish. We could always catch fish.

This was Merry's idea and it meant that we could occasionally take off from work and explore or go swimming and picnic upstream. It gave us a break from our usual routine of unending work, we always felt better after a day of doing only what we felt like doing.

We had tried to keep the signal fire burning on the plateau but often forgot it for days. One day, while carrying wood to the top of our cliff, we decided it might be to our advantage to explore on the western side. Actually our cliff was a ridge, not terribly tall, and we lived on the steep eastern face of it. The other side was gently sloping, with some trees and an easy descent.

After we had stacked our wood, we walked hand-in-hand down the hill, picking our way along the easiest path. Many times we had used the binoculars to look over the terrain but had not seen anything more than we saw on the eastern side. One area looked kind of different but we couldn't make out details because of surrounding trees. It seemed to be only a couple of miles distant, so we headed towards it, taking our time and looking for edible goodies as we ambled along. We had no fears about getting lost. Our ridge was behind us and stretched for many miles . . . no way to lose it.

It was to prove an eventful day. The weather was beautiful, not hot or cold, just brisk enough that walking was exhilarating.

I was armed, of course. Merry wanted to know why I had the slingshot in my hip pocket, the knife and hatchet in my belt and my spear in the hand not holding hers. "The better to protect you, my dear," I told her.

"From what?"

"From whatever," I answered.

Actually, I hadn't seen any ferocious animals. No dinosaurs. The largest was a deer I had stunned with a huge stone from my slingshot. Because I kept my knife honed to a razor edge, killing the deer had taken only a moment. I had saved the skin and Merry helped me stretch it between poles. In my mind I saw it as a rug for our floor, nice to walk on and rather stylish. My idea was great, Merry told me later, but I needed to work on it a little more. The skin was stiff, hard as rock, and stank.

"I think you have to tan it," she advised, holding her nose.

Not caring if I appeared ignorant, I asked her how she'd go about it, if she was so smart.

"If you want me to tell you how to do it, ask politely."

So I kissed her nose and asked her, humbly, how to tan a deer hide, please.

"I haven't the faintest notion," she said.

But she helped me move the hide downwind, both of us hoping in vain that time would soften it and the weather would help out with the smell.

The possibility that another deer would appear was reason enough to keep my weapons handy. But most of all I had to protect her. I would protect her with my life, with my dying breath, if it came to that.

I loved her with a feeling so strong that just saying "I love you" didn't come close to expressing it. I knew she loved me when we were making love, an activity she enjoyed as much as I did, but it was the time in between when she showed me how much. So I carried my weapons and she teased me about them but we knew it was something I had to do for both of us.

In less than an hour of easy walking, we had reached the place that looked different from the cliff top. It *was* different. It was a huge swamp.

There were tall trees growing in the water with cattails in abundance around the shallow edges. I was elated! "Merry, just wait till you taste what I can do with cattails! We can eat almost every part." My impulse was to take back huge bundles but we remembered how far we had to walk so we settled on one good-sized armload each.

"I'll bet there are crawfish and who knows what other great things!"

"Maybe snakes?" Merry was afraid of snakes, though we had not seen any.

"No, no snakes," I promised her. "Tomorrow I'll come back and look around."

"Not without me, you don't!"

Now that we knew our true feelings for each other, we were seldom apart. More often than not, Merry would be with me when I hunted or fished, activities that took many hours. I didn't like to be any distance away from her, either.

If the day sounds idyllic, it was. We were full of breakfast, the August sun was warm on our backs, we were safe, the weather was perfect and we were so very much in love.

Walking back we both heard the noise. Something was thrashing about in the underbrush a few feet from us. We stopped dead still. I dropped my cattails and lifted my spear. Cautiously I moved closer, Merry a step behind me.

We both laughed when we saw the cause of such a huge commotion. A tiny pig was caught in a tangle of roots, almost yanking its hind leg off trying to escape. I had an instant vision of frying bacon.

"Poor dear thing," Merry cried. "Hurry, Chris, help it!"

"Help it? We're going to eat it!"

But at Merry's urging I untangled the animal and handed it to her. "Its mama probably left it when it couldn't get free," I said.

"Poor lost baby," Merry crooned, cradling the frightened pig in her arms. The poor baby grunted a few times, looking at Merry and rolling its eyes. She cuddled it closer and patted its head. The eyes rolled some more.

"You take my cattails, darling," she told me, "I'll carry the pig."

So the three of us went home, me staggering under a mountain of cattails, Merry walking ahead carrying the pig.

"Pigs are very smart and clean, too," she informed me as she bathed the squirming animal. "We'll keep her inside with us."

I told her that just because we slept on the floor we did not have to lie with pigs.

"We're not lying with pigs," she sniffed. "It's only one tiny little pig and I'll make it a bed of its own."

So Aroma — for that is what Merry named her — was now an accredited member of the household with all of the privileges of the other members.

She was brownish-colored with some dark bristly hair around her neck and on her head. Her leg was bruised, not cut or broken, and she limped for only a few days. True to Merry's prediction, she was very clean. She had no odor that I could detect but she would often sniff my feet and ankles and grunt in disgust, coughing piggishly to express disapproval. That she lived indoors with us was a fact we soon accepted without question, all three of us.

Aroma ate with the appetite of ten. She instantly consumed whatever we had left from our meals, a considered blessing because we had no refrigeration. Occasionally some of our smoked fish and meat rotted and Aroma would dispatch great quantities with squeals of satisfaction. Thereafter, she would roll her eyes appreciatively when we passed the tiny smokehouse I had built near the stream.

That she was in love with Merry was very clear. She dogged Mary's footsteps outdoors and followed Merry with her eyes when we were inside. I could not fault her for that good judgment.

She had her sleeping quarters on the opposite side of the room near the kitchen and she usually retired earlier than we did. Occasionally, when we were making too much noise for her, she'd sit up and grunt at us a few times. On these occasions she was ignored.

* * * * *

The VW was a skeleton now. We had taken from it everything that we could possibly use and so it sat, abandoned. Six months of rain and sun had caused rust to form on the parts not protected by paint.

One of the most useful items it provided was our winter stove. Using the doors, the hood, and various other smooth metal parts that I could shape with the hatchet, I constructed a metal fireplace, one that gave off a cozy glow, didn't burn wood too fast and didn't take up much room. We considered using it as a cook stove too, but the clay and rock stove we had first built had proved to be an excellent appliance. In winter we could probably use two stoves, anyway.

One benefit our cave provided was a gentle updraft that exited all smoke someplace overhead. No matter what choking clouds our fires sometimes caused, the suction wafted all of it up and away.

We had placed our cook stove in the center of the larger end of our room, our washing and cleaning area (our kitchen) to the right against the wall and storage shelves to the left of that. Our small dining table and two chairs were in the center of the room, our sofa and the two VW bucket seats against the left wall, and our new stove sat in the middle of the floor, between our bed and the rest of the room. The bathroom opening was at the foot of our bed and the door to the ramp was at mid-point on the outside wall.

Placed here and there along the walls were the vases Merry had made for decoration. I had built low tables for them and Merry kept them filled with green things or dried things or even flowers, when flowers were available. Some were used as planters and, in spite of the low light level, we had greenery growing.

Our prized possession was the spiral notebook, two short pencils and a ball-point pen found in the VW glove compartment.

Clean clothes were folded and kept on a shelf by the bed. We could see that clothing would eventually prove to be a problem. Merry's camping gear had contained a small sewing kit with a package of needles and some brightly colored thread so she did what she could to keep us adequately covered. The stitching she pulled out of the VW seats was some sort of plastic and proved more durable than ordinary thread. But our things were wearing out in spite of all the stitching and patching.

Our success with animal hides was zero. No one could have worn the skins we tried to cure. We scraped then soaked the skins in the stream; they turned to slime. We scraped and stretched the hides on limbs and they dried so hard we could have worn them as snowshoes. Some rotted and the fur fell off, others shrank and cracked. All of them smelled. We kept trying, however, and hoped that one day we would hit upon the means to turn out something soft and supple that we could wear. I told Merry that Eskimo women chewed the skins until they were conditioned for clothing. She said that she would rather wear leaves!

My tennis shoes had almost dissolved from being so wet so much, as had Merry's, but the hiking boots were still in good condition although our socks were worn out at heel and toe. Merry could no longer repair them, so used the unworn parts as patches for other things.

We were pitiful looking in our ragged, patched clothing but we were clean, Merry saw to that!

Chapter XIII

It was just daylight, Merry had two torches burning brightly at the kitchen end of our room. I was standing by our stove, waiting for the fire to burn down into coals. I poked at the wood and watched sparks and smoke spiral upward, disappearing into the ceiling of our cave. I said idly, "Where do you think the smoke goes?"

Merry turned from the sink and smiled at me. She looked at the ceiling for a moment. "I think it goes into one of those cracks." Still smiling she turned back to the sink and our breakfast preparations.

"Where does it go after it goes into the cracks?" Then I added, "I've never seen smoke coming out of the top of the ridge so it must travel horizontally and then come out in some other place. Farther down the line, I mean. It has to go somewhere, doesn't it? And I'd like to know where, that's all."

"If it's important to you we'll go look for the smoke after breakfast, okay?"

"Well, not really that important. We can do it some other time, I guess." I poked the fire a couple of times and saw that it was glowing red, just right for cooking. "Your fire's ready, hon, shall I heat more water for tea?"

"Please. But first feed Aroma, will you?"

Aroma was sitting in front of her food basket, grunting softly, waiting for one of us to open it so that she could begin her morning properly. I pulled the latch, opened the lid, and took out a handful of berries. Aroma grunted at my stinginess so I added another handful to her plate.

Then, laughing because our mornings were so predictable, I walked to the door opening and breathed deeply of the clean, cool September air. I had chopped wood all day yesterday and, exhausted, had fallen into bed right after supper. It felt good to be rested.

Merry planned to fire the pots she had made for carrying water, starting early this morning, and she needed a lot of wood for her kiln. It had to be of a certain size in order to fit into the fire pit so I had trimmed and shortened what seemed like a thousand miles of wood. We would find our wood on the forest floor and drag or carry home whatever we could handle and then it would take hours of labor to turn it into the right size for our stoves. I think I would have given almost anything for a wood-chopping axe.

Merry wanted to help with the trimming but I was afraid she'd hurt herself, flailing away with our tiny hatchet, so I insisted on doing that part even though I had never used a hatchet in my life until we landed here.

Already we had to go farther and farther each time to collect our wood. There was no danger of running out but it would be great to have some kind of cart to help with the hauling. I was surprised that Merry hadn't asked for one.

"Come eat, sweetie."

I turned from the door, looking at my Merry in the sunlight that now streamed through the opening, and at our cheery table.

"Pour the tea, will you hon?"

Merry served our plates and I poured the tea and we sat at our table and ate breakfast. Merry seemed as cheerful as always; we talked about the kiln and today's firing and how long it was going to take and how successful it would probably be. She hoped to finish before dark, allowing the kiln to cool slowly overnight. Merry urged me to eat another helping. On the surface, everything was fine but I sensed something was not right with her.

After I had collapsed on the bed last night Merry had stayed up for a while, leafing through one of the field guides until the torches probably burned down. I hadn't come fully awake when she came to bed but I'd felt her lean over me to adjust the cover then lightly touch her lips to mine. "Goodnight my darling," she had whispered, "I love you." Then she'd gotten under the cover and snuggled by my side. So, everything had been fine up to that point.

As I ate my breakfast I watched Merry ignoring hers. I was thinking that just because I loved her more than life, I didn't have the right to pick at her every thought and mood. Whatever was wrong, I had best let it be for now.

"Merry, there's something wrong, isn't there? Please tell me what it is." So much for good intentions!

She took in a deep breath, letting the worry show. "I didn't think you knew," she said slowly. "There was an . . . an earthquake last night."

I almost dropped my cup. "An earthquake?" I repeated. "Here?"

"You were sleeping like the dead, hon, and I didn't think it woke you but the ground shook and the walls . . . you didn't see all the soot everywhere this morning?"

I looked around. I guess there was more than the usual film of black here and there but nothing that you wouldn't expect to find in a cave that had fires burning most of the time. I had not put on my shoes so I inspected the bottom of my feet. Very black. Knowing how often Merry swept, I was convinced.

"How could there be an earthquake and me not know it?"

"When you're as tired as you were last night, Gabriel could blow and you wouldn't hear. It wasn't a major quake, darling, it only lasted a few seconds. But I felt little pieces of the ceiling fall and my dishes rattled." She grinned at me. "You grunted and turned over and took all the cover. But you do that anyway, even when there isn't any earthquake."

I held her hand in mine, my thoughts whirling a mile a minute. "Do you think we should move out of here? What if it happens again and the whole ceiling drops? We'd be squashed like bugs . . . there'd be no way to dig ourselves out from under all this rock . . . supposing, even, that we were alive!"

Merry interrupted my hysterics. "We've been here for almost seven months now and this is the first time. Maybe it won't happen again."

A picture of our ramp flashed in my head. Sure of my facts, I said, "But it has happened before, you know. Look at our ramp! It was a piece of cliff that shook loose in a quake, I'd bet on it! I think we should build a shelter in the open. We don't want to get trapped in here!" I looked around at the rock walls closing in on me. I had visions of Merry buried under a pile of stone and me, flattened under another pile, unable to reach her. It was so real that my insides started churning. I had thought we were safe in our cave and now it was going to fall and crush us as we slept and I was powerless to do anything to stop it.

"Calm down, you're getting too upset, honey!"

"Of course I'm upset, aren't you?"

"I wasn't until you were. I almost wish I hadn't said anything. Have some more tea and then we'll go out and build the fire in our kiln."

I was not to be distracted. "Merry, I can't let anything happen to you." I was going to say more but my voice failed.

She put the pot back on the stove then stood next to me, her arms circling my shoulders, her cheek pressed to the top of my head. "Nothing's going to happen to me. It's you I worry about."

I turned and buried my face in her softness. I smelled the clean, sun-dried odor of her shirt, felt her warmth as she tightened her arms, pressing me closer. And in that moment I felt more helpless than I ever had in my life. It was for this reason, I guess, that my eyes brimmed with tears. That, and knowing that in spite of anything I could do, I could not protect us from an earthquake.

Crying is not an easy thing for me to do. I try to hold back, thinking that tears are not helpful in solving the problem that caused them. Crying at this point would not stop an earthquake or make us safe if one shattered our world so I took in a very deep breath, fighting for control. I would have made it, too, except Merry, kissing the top of my head, said, "There, there, darling. It'll be okay. We're going to be just fine." She tightened her arms and hugged me to her, patting my back and shoulders.

At those words I quit trying and let the tears flow. Merry held me, her arms tight, as I wailed against her shirt front. I wanted to tell her that I loved her, that I would be strong and take care of her if an earthquake came, that I would do anything, give my life if necessary, to keep her safe and well. With great effort, I finally managed to stop the flow. "Merry," I said hoarsely, "I don't know what happened to me. I didn't mean to cry."

"I know, darling, I know." Tenderly, she wiped my face with a napkin. "You are always so brave and you take such good care of us."

"Look who's taking care of who," I managed between sniffs, trying to clear my nose. I frowned when I saw her shirt front soaked with my tears. "I won't let you down like that again," I promised.

"Oh, my baby, don't say that! You never have, ever let me down!"

"I guess I did sound like a baby, huh." I looked into her beautiful eyes, now level with mine as she knelt by my chair. Then I realized, "You've never called me that before."

There was an impish grin on her face. "I haven't called you that aloud, no. In this family of two, I'm the baby and you've always been the grownup." Her grin widened. "But to myself, I've always called you that."

"Say it again."

"Baby," she crooned softly, touching my face with her finger tips, "baby, baby, baby."

I kissed her then. I pulled her face to mine and I kissed her with all the love I had for her. It was a kiss that lasted and lasted.

"Ahhh, baby," she breathed when I moved my mouth from hers.

"Oh, baby, baby," she moaned softly some time later. Then louder, "Chris, baby! Oh, Chris!" Finally, slow and dreamy, "Baby, my sweet baby, I love you so."

* * * * *

Since the morning was now mostly gone, we decided to start early tomorrow on the pottery. Today we would look for smoke.

Merry had said that the best way to make smoke was to burn oil so we poured a precious cupful on the wood burning in the stove, then walked to the cliff top. Aroma came with us, snorting and grunting happily.

Ten minutes or so later, after we had seen no sign, I walked down to the cave. The fire was still burning merrily, sending up a pillar of choking black smoke which disappeared into the ceiling. I climbed the ramp again.

"There's plenty of fire and smoke, Merry, and it's all going up into the ceiling." I looked all along the ridge. "I don't see any sign of it coming out anyplace."

"Where there's smoke there's smoke and," she added, grinning and looking straight up at me, "where there's fire . . ." She left the sentence unfinished, raising her eyebrows slightly and I felt myself blush.

Crying had a cathartic effect, I found. The weighty things I worried about — Merry, food, illness, winter, rescue, and now earthquakes, to name but a few — had faded with the tears this morning, and I had made love to Merry over and over. "You should cry more often, baby," she had whispered to me.

I stomped to where she was sitting and frowned down at her. "Madam," I announced, "there's more fire where that came from and if you keep looking at me like that you're likely to spend the entire day in bed! Now, put that pig down and follow me!"

"Methinks," Merry said to Aroma as she dumped the animal unceremoniously off her lap, "methinks I have created a baby monster." Then, pulling my head down, she whispered in my ear, "But I love you anyway."

— 111 —

Hand-in-hand we walked north along the ridge. Using the binoculars we could see for a good distance but there was no sign of smoke. Finally we turned and walked south, passing our ramp on the way. Still no smoke.

"It doesn't have to exit, you know," Merry said, "it may hang up in a crack or in a lot of cracks and not come out at all. This entire ridge is honeycombed with cracks and probably more caves than the one we're using." She was thinking hard, as interested in finding the smoke as I was. "As a matter of fact, I've often wondered about our stream of water. Chris, have you ever thought about how it flows through our bathroom?"

I had to admit that I hadn't.

"Well, think about a stream of water flowing through rock twenty feet or more higher than ground level. We've never seen where it comes from or where it goes, have we?"

"No," I admitted, "but you're the teacher. Give me a clue."

"It's from an underground spring, sweetie, nothing more or less."

"Ah ha! So it wells up from the ground, snakes it way along the inside of the ridge, then finds an exit and joins the outside stream further south, right?"

"Give my baby an A plus." And she wrote it in the air. "Now, for the final exam. Did you look at the water this morning?"

Again, I had to admit that I hadn't. I had used the bathroom but I wasn't paying much attention to the water. It was there, it was flowing and that's all I'd noticed.

"You should have, sweetie, because it's changed. When we go back you'll see that it's dirtier than ever and isn't nearly as deep as it has been."

"How come?" I really wanted to know.

"Promise you'll stay calm?" At my nod, she continued, "The quake must have caused part of the cliff to fall into the path of the stream somewhere north of our place because it's carrying so much more debris than it usually does. And now the stream has to find its way around the obstruction and make another channel. It may have made a couple of channels because what's left of our stream has a slower, much shallower flow."

"But it's always had stuff floating in it, Merry. So maybe this isn't the first time part of the ridge has caved in." Talking about our ridge caving in made me shudder.

"I've always thought that," Merry confessed. "Underground streams are usually crystal clear according to what I've read so I kind of thought that some, ah, something had to have partially dammed it. Lately I've even seen green leaves floating by and that made me realize that some leaves and things from the top of the cliff must be washing down into the stream through a crack in the cliff. Probably when it rains."

"Honey, I'm amazed."

"Amazed at what? That I've thought about our stream? She hugged my arm. "Still water runs deep, they say." Her laughter was bright and clear and I laughed with her.

The sun was past straight up and I was hungry. We had a canteen of tea but I wanted food. "Let's go back, okay? I haven't seen any sign of smoke and we've walked miles."

Merry looked back for Aroma who had given up long before. "All right," she said, turning, "let's go home."

I went instantly to the bathroom and confirmed what Merry had said. "If this stream ever clears," I told her, "we could have water to drink and bathe. We wouldn't have to haul it anymore." I was thinking of the thousand trips I had made.

"No, darling, it'll probably take more years than we have to clear our stream. In all likelihood there'll be more cave-ins with each tremor." She grimaced, realizing she'd said more than she intended.

She was at the sink and I turned her to face me. "Please share with me, Merry. I promise to share with you, no matter what. I know there'll be more quakes but we'll make it. Together." And I hugged her to me.

* * * * *

That night I lay awake. The last few live coals created a halo of soft amber over our stove. As I watched the glow fade I felt darkness settle against my length; a weight without substance, heavy, icy, unrelieved by light or sound.

This valley is going to kill us, I thought, and I'm scared.

Sighing, I leaned into Merry's sleeping form, taking comfort from her warmth.

Chapter XIV

We had not yet decided what we could do to prepare for winter but we both knew that we would be spending it here, in this valley.

"Coats," Merry said. "We'll each need a coat for winter and I know where we'll get them." She pointed to our bed. "We can cover the straw with a sheet and use the bottom bag as our blanket and the top bag for our coats." An awesome task to my eyes.

Merry was meticulous in whatever she did and she took many, many measurements from each of us with her home-made yardstick. On a notebook page she wrote each figure next to a rough sketch of the coat. Her drawings to the contrary, the coats, when finished, were beautiful, snug, and mostly fit. Plastic stitching from the VW held the garment together and each coat had an outside pocket of terry cloth towel.

"Wood," Merry said, "we'll need plenty of wood. And I'd like to have a door to close. Not only will it make our house more private but it'll keep out some of the cold."

I could not see how we could be any more private than in a concealed hole in the side of a cliff but the wind might be a factor in the winter I conceded, and a door would help keep out both wind and cold. So I built a door of thin poles, lashing them together with wire. I also put in a glass pane from the side wing of a VW door. I jammed a thick tree trunk from floor to ceiling on one side of the opening and used wire to hang our door from that upright pole. For a while I toyed with the idea of using the actual VW door hinges but I couldn't get them off the VW and had no way of securing them to the wall anyway.

Our door opened and closed as neatly as any other except that it didn't swing as freely as a real door and it sagged a little and may have had a gap or two here and there. But on the whole it was quite snug. It did make us feel we had more privacy. After we had gone inside for the night, we'd close our door and secure it with the log I used as a prop. If we heard knocking, we could look out the glass without opening the door and see who had come visiting.

"This is real uptown," Merry purred as she snuggled close to me that night. "I can kiss you and do all sorts of things and nobody can see."

"Ah," I said, turning my body to rest on top of hers, "let's try a few of those things and see if anybody's watching."

* * * * *

One day Merry said, "You have to build a smoker, Chris, so we can make jerky."

I knew how to smoke meat and was very proud of the small smoker we had built out of thick logs some months back and the tasty meat we had smoked. "You want something bigger?" I knew in her mind she had something the size of a grain silo.

"Just a little so we can prepare plenty of good things for the winter."

I was afraid to ask but I did. "Show me how much bigger you want it."

It took two weeks to build but we could have smoked an elephant in it. The hard work was in hauling enough logs to make our new smoker wider at the base and tall enough to stand in. We had already hacked apart most of the fallen wood near us so we had to go farther into the woods to find the right size; not too big around and at least ten feet tall. Since we didn't have any competition for the limbs on the forest floor it was mostly a matter of search and drag.

We kept the same tepee shape as in our first smoker so construction was a matter of leaning the logs against one another at the top and wiring them together. We chinked the gaps with clay and moss, left nine of the uprights loose to be removed as a door and scraped out a shallow fire pit in the center. Now, instead of drying a few animals and fish from time to time, I had to work hard to catch enough to fill the cross bars so the effort of collecting wood wouldn't be wasted.

We had no idea how long we'd be confined to the cave, surviving on whatever we had stored, so we kept the fire smoldering. In the absence of salt, smoking was the only way I could think of to preserve fish and meat. It was even harder work to haul enough of the dense, oak-like wood that burned for so long but we kept hauling and burning.

"It would certainly save time and effort if we had salt. While you're out hunting look around for some, will you?" Merry had said.

"Would you like Morton's or will the store brand do?"

"If you're going to talk smart, there'll be no TV for you tonight. Or," she added sweetly, "whatever it is we do instead of watching TV."

A fate worse than death.

* * * * *

In the woods near the deep part of the stream were grapevines that had grown to cover the nearby shrubs and trees. As the weeks passed, I watched the tiny green pin heads grow into dark brownish-purple fruit. They had thick skins and huge seeds — but they were grapes, sweet and juicy.

In late August, as they ripened I'd bring bunches to Merry and we'd sit and pop the grapes into our mouths, letting the juice run down our chins. It was so good to taste their sweetness.

"Wouldn't wine be nice, my love?" Merry asked.

"Certainly, dear, would you like sweet or dry, white or red..."

Merry cut me off by saying in her softest voice, "Remember the TV..."

So I hurried off to collect grapes.

* * * * *

My notion of wine making was that you crush the grapes with your feet while singing something in Italian. Then somebody else makes the wine. I must have been right because what I came up with was more vinegar than anything else.

"Lo, how the mighty have fallen," I told her as we sipped the liquid. "I think I left out something."

"You are still wonderful in my eyes," she soothed me. "Think how good this will taste on the greens. It'll be like down-home southern cooking, without the cornbread, however." And she filled her spoon again.

It was not even good vinegar but it was a new taste and one we continued to enjoy.

It was Merry who thought about boiling eggs and letting them sit in the vinegar. "I think I saw this in a bar once," she told me. So, when eggs were available again, we tried it and thereafter enjoyed pickled eggs with our meals and as a snack.

The real find of the century was honey. I heard the bees before I saw them, their angry humming causing me to leave the path and search for the sound. The bees were swarming around a fallen tree, a hollow one in which they had made their enormous hive. Heavy evening winds had probably knocked the tree to the ground and the bees didn't know what to do.

I, however, did know what to do.

I walked back home and grabbed what I needed. Merry was busy with her kiln and merely waved. On the way back to the fallen tree I made a torch, using a piece of tire, some stuffing from the VW seats and engine oil. When I focused the sun's rays through my eyeglass lens the torch caught instantly and burned with thick black smoke. Hoping the rubber smell wouldn't ruin the honey, I advanced on the tree with the torch in front of me.

The bees fought a good fight but my advanced technology was too much for them. I emerged as the owner of a tree full of honey.

I scooped enough honey to fill the bowl I'd brought with me after taking one tiny taste of the golden liquid to make sure the smoke hadn't ruined it. Later, after Merry had gone inside for the evening, I hid the bowl in our hallway.

Merry had prepared a delicious supper of meat stew with potatoes and gravy, onions and tasty greens from our garden, and yams. The yams were actually a thick orange root of some plant that was delicious and sweet when baked in the coals. And, of course, we had hot tea.

When she served our plates, I acted as if I heard our turkeys squawking and opened the door, pretending to listen. Merry's back was to me and she didn't see me bring in the bowl of honey.

With a flourish, I spooned honey onto her yams and some into her tea. She watched, eyes wide with astonishment and then with delight. She clapped her hands but then started crying.

I knelt by her chair. "Merry, darling, don't cry."

"I'm crying because I'm happy!"

I put my finger into the honey bowl then stuck it in her mouth. "Well, eat honey while you cry."

We both ate honey that night. We ate it on our yams, on our fish, drank it in our tea and licked it from our spoons and fingers. We were almost covered with it by the time our meal was done.

After we had gorged, Merry told me, "Now, my little old winemaker, I think you have the ingredients to make my Chablis."

I probably did at that.

We had a lovely evening. We sat and talked, ate honey off our spoons and fingers and talked some more. We told each other how each of us had lived before, in that other time. Again, I told Merry about Candy, everything I could remember. Then she wanted me to tell how I had fallen in love with her that night at Sylvia's. So I told her that again, too.

She talked about her two lesbian love affairs, the first in summer camp and the second, which lasted two years, during college. "Once I knew what was happening, I tried my darnedest to be the normal person my family thought I was." She smiled ruefully. "I told you about my marriage. It would have been funny if it hadn't been so frightening . . . I knew the minute I said I do that I really didn't! That I never could! Darling, I was trying so hard to be the straight person I pretended to be. It was only after we became friends and after I began to want you so much that I knew I couldn't deny my feelings any longer."

I dipped my spoon into the honey bowl. "Merry, I love you so much. I'd rather be with you, here in this place, than . . ."

Merry leaned and touched my cheek with her sticky fingers. "I love you the most," she whispered, her smile tender.

I know how to define happiness. In spite of having more than our share of hardships, I was happy. I also know the meaning of the saying about a cup running over. My cup was filled with happiness, it spilled over into everything I did.

I saw our world with two sets of eyes now, one pair of eyes colored by the power of my love for Merry and her love for me, and everything in view was beautiful. Those eyes saw a landscape generous with color and texture, bountiful in every way. The other pair of eyes belonged to the pragmatists that I am. I saw the harshness and cruelty of our world, the road of unending physical toil. Frail as we were, we coped with our existence on a superficial level. Our buoy was our courage and our love; that alone sustained us.

But tonight I put my fears behind me. We were full, the fire was warm and our cave was cozy.

I bathed and went to bed first. Full of honey and good food, tired from the physical labors of the day, I dozed waiting for Merry.

I was aware that she had pulled the top cover down and thought she was getting into bed. Instead, I felt her touching my breast. Smelling the sweetness of honey, I opened my eyes.

She began coating my breasts with honey from my special cup. Slowly, she would dip and rub, dip and rub. She touched me nowhere else. Then she lay beside me, propped on an elbow, and very, very slowly slid her honey-covered fingers into me. Then she leaned over and began licking the honey from my breasts. Neither of us had said a word.

I tried not to move as she licked in circles, her tongue not touching my nipples which were rock hard now. She did not move her fingers but held them immobile inside me. Unable to hold still, I moved my hips but felt no answering movement from her hand, just a steady, even pressure like her steady, even licking.

She finished the left breast, except for the nipple, then began licking circles around the right. I could not help moving my hips; they moved of their own accord. I wanted to feel her fingers as they slipped in and out; I wanted the thickness of the honey to mix with my own flooding moisture and I imagined feeling the movement of her hand. But she held her hand steady, not moving, holding very still in spite of my groans.

I became aware that the circling of her tongue had stopped and I lay still for the moment, not knowing what was to come. Then she lowered her mouth again and began sucking honey from a nipple. Slowly at first and gently, she sucked, making little noises with her mouth as her fingers began moving, also slowly and gently, the heel of her hand pressing lightly but keeping contact as her fingers moved.

She moved on to the other nipple, still honey coated, and took it into her mouth, pulling upward gently with her teeth. Then the gentleness stopped. Her breath rasping, she began sucking greedily, almost gnawing, and I felt pain as her teeth closed, not gently at all!

Her hand began moving with a fierceness she had never shown before. It took only a few seconds to bring me to a shuddering climax. The echoes of my cries still bounding from wall to wall, I lay breathless, heart thudding.

She kissed me then and I tasted honey. "This," she said, "is how I thank you for your surprise."

Still faint, my head reeling, I silently vowed to look for salt tomorrow.

Chapter XV

It had rained during the night. I stood in the doorway, yawning, looking out over our domain at our fresh, crisp green garden and wondering, as I had so many times before, how many millions of years it would take to level the mountains that surrounded us.

The turkeys were already up and searching the ground. They wasted a lot of time looking for food on the barren area just below our ramp. The earth there was covered with coarse gravel and no edible greenery that I could see. They found the few withered leaves I had thrown down last night and pecked cautiously. Not eating, testing — as I had last night. I had to smile.

I had continued to look for plants to use as tobacco. Why not? When dried many of the leaves in our valley smelled like stale cigars. So, not quite cured of the cigarette habit, I tried smoking the ones that did not smell too frightful.

Last night, as before, Merry had watched with amusement as I carefully rolled a dried leaf into a tube of the right size. "I have to see this," she murmured as I put a glowing brand to the end and puffed . . . and puffed. Some minutes later, almost cross-eyed and certainly dizzy, I gave up. "If it won't burn I can't smoke it, can I?" I had asked rhetorically. "No," Merry answered, "thank goodness."

Some movement of mine caught the turkeys' attention and they stretched their necks and started talking to me, asking for the breakfast goodies that we usually saved for them. This morning I had very little. Aroma had feasted on the leftovers last night, leaving nothing for the birds. I dropped a handful of berries down to them and promised them more later in the day. After breakfast I planned to go to the swamp for cattails and to check my nets. I reminded myself to take along baskets that I could fill with the orange fruit the turkeys liked so much.

"Chris?" It was Merry calling me to breakfast. I took a final look around then turned and walked carefully back into our cave because I wasn't wearing shoes and my feet were still tender enough to resent the rough rock floor.

Merry was standing in front of the stove frying potato pancakes. Next to scrambled eggs I liked these best. She fried them thin and crisp, and when I floated them in honey I could eat almost a dozen. The potatoes weren't really potatoes like those we were used to because they were long and thin instead of fat and round but they had the same taste and consistency.

I walked up behind Merry and hugged her around the waist and kissed her neck. The wooden spatula still in her hand, she turned in my arms. I kissed her eyes and then her mouth. She was so soft and warm against me that I kissed her again. Her arms tightened around me and our next kiss was long and serious.

"Woah, hoss," Merry breathed when I lifted my mouth from hers, "do you want pancakes or kisses?"

I grinned down at her and pretended to be thinking. "Pancakes," I said, "I'll take pancakes."

Merry turned back to the stove. "Ha, you'd better want pancakes! You got more than your share of kisses last night!"

While we were eating Aroma wandered in and sat on the floor next to Merry. Aroma was allowed to sit under or near the table while we were eating but she was not allowed to beg for food so she had learned to sit quietly, usually leaning against Mary's chair, grunting discreetly to remind us of her presence.

I said, "We may have caught something in those nets I set out in the swamp. If I'm right we'll have crawfish for supper tonight."

"Do you suppose I should stew them or should they be fried?"

"From what I remember you boil them, heads and all. We'll throw some of those spicy leaves and things in the pot to add to the flavor. Haven't you ever had boiled seafood?"

Merry shook her head. "No, but I'm willing to try. What would you say if we looked for a turtle, too?"

She collected our dishes and put them in the sink. Behind her back I made a face. I liked turtle stew and turtle steaks but I didn't enjoy killing turtles. I didn't really enjoy killing any of the animals we ate but I did what had to be done. It was just that turtles were so slow it seemed somehow unfair to catch them. This peculiarity of mine wouldn't stop me if a turtle happened our way so I told Merry that, yes, we'd look for one.

After I helped Merry wash dishes, I collected my weapons and put on my boots. I made a nest of baskets, the third and smallest one with a lid to keep the crawfish from getting loose.

Sipping another cup of tea, I watched Merry change from shorts to jeans. She wore thongs made from tire rubber and inner tube pieces. She had made a pair for me, too, but the rubber between my toes was uncomfortable so I wore them briefly and only while I was inside.

The three of us climbed the ramp to the top of the cliff then began walking towards the swamp, following a straight path that led us past the trees with the bitter orange fruit. As we walked, I bent to pick up smooth round stones for my slingshot. Carrying stones in my pockets had seriously thinned the fabric of my jeans and poked a few holes here and there so Merry had added patches made from the headliner of the VW. She had also patched my knees and my seat and made a draw-string bag for the stones so as to save what was left of my pants. It was not always comfortable to have a bag of rocks tied to my belt and flapping against my leg but I didn't dare complain. Merry said I looked poor but respectable. I thought poor and funny was more like it.

When we reached the fruit trees we left Aroma. She was fond of some wiggly things she found in the ground under these particular trees and would spend the morning happily rooting and eating.

It was a pleasant walk to the swamp and when we reached the water I saw that all of my nets were still in place. I could find them easily because I had tied a little leafy branch to each of the wires that stuck up above the water.

I sat on the log we had pulled close to the water's edge and took off my boots. Merry stood in the shallow water and held the basket and I waded out to the first net. I picked it up expecting to see crawfish but there was nothing in it, not even the bait.

All of the nets were empty and all of the bait was gone. Merry frowned when I showed her the empty nets. "What took the bait, do you suppose?"

I shrugged. "Maybe alligators. Maybe a swamp demon. I wouldn't be surprised at either."

Merry raised her eyebrows at me. "Maybe a turtle? They're omnivorous, aren't they?"

I agreed but I didn't think anything really big had eaten the bait because the nets weren't moved. I thought it more likely that tiny mouths had nibbled the bait away over the days since I'd set the traps. I had brought a supply of animal entrails so I sat on the log and began tying the new bait to the nets.

Merry watched me thoughtfully for a few minutes. "Chris, I think I know why we didn't catch anything."

I was dripping water and mud and mess all over my lap and hands. I knew she was going to tell me something simple and very obvious and that I should have thought of it first. "Why," I asked, "why do you think I didn't catch anything?"

"Because we left the nets here for two days. Whatever it was had plenty of time to finish dinner and scram. I think we should bait the nets, hang around for a little while, then see if we've caught anything."

How simple and how obvious. I noticed her saying "we" did this and "we" should do that and I loved her so much for not wanting to make me feel dumb that I laughed out loud. "If I wasn't such a mess I'd hug you! Of course, that's why the nets were empty. Merry you're a genius!" I meant it, too.

"There's one more thing, Chris. I think we'll scare away whatever it is when we wade out to pick up the net. What if we put the nets closer to shore and use a long pole to pick them up. That way, whatever it is wouldn't see us coming . . ."

Before she finished I had the hatchet in my hand and was looking for a tall, thin tree. It only took a few minutes to find and cut just the right one.

"Hon," I said, "as long as we have to hang around we could explore the other side of the swamp. Would you like to?"

Merry opened our canteen and handed it to me. "I'd love to go exploring with you."

So, after I washed and we'd both had a few swallows of tea, we set out around the pond. Merry's hand in mine, we made our way along the water's edge, me walking barefoot on the water side and Merry sloshing along beside me in her thongs. We didn't find anything different from what we'd seen already but I was glad to see so many cattails growing in clumps here and there. I was going to chop an armload, then decided to wait until we were closer to our nets. Cattails are spindly but it doesn't take many to make a heavy pile.

We kept walking, making squishy sounds with our feet. The mud was soft and I often sank to my ankles. I was trying to avoid limbs concealed under the slush so I wasn't striding hard like I usually did. Even so, whatever it was I stepped on was sharp and I jerked my foot up.

"Stepped on a limb?"

I stood on one leg, balanced on Merry, and examined the bottom of my foot. "I don't think so. Damn thing was sharp as a knife."

"Are you bleeding?" Merry was concerned, trying to see the bottom of my foot.

I decided I wasn't hurt. "Well no, but I'm going to see whatever it was!"

I bent and stuck my hand in the shallow water. My fingers found something with good finger holds so I grasped and yanked hard, wondering what it could possibly be. It came out of the mud so fast I almost fell over backward. Merry grabbed me and I floundered for a few seconds until I got my balance. Then we looked at what I had in my hand.

Merry gasped and clutched my arm tighter. My fingers flew open and it dropped from my hand, splashing mud when it landed.

It was a human skull. A skull minus the lower jaw but definitely a skull and definitely human. I don't know how long we stood there, Merry clutching my arm, staring down at the empty eye sockets that stared back at us, rivulets of slimy mud clinging to the bone.

"Oh, no!" Merry moaned. "Oh, no!" Her grasp was cutting off circulation in my arm.

I bent to pick it up again.

"Don't, Chris. Leave it!"

"I can't, Merry. I have to . . ." By now I had the skull in my hand again, close enough to see it clearly. I felt my breakfast moving towards my throat. I swallowed hard and took a deep breath.

Merry turned her head away. I knew she had seen what I saw. Some of the teeth were missing but several of the ones still attached to the skull had fillings in them. Silver filings in the back and one of gold in the front.

The pancakes moved higher. I breathed harder.

I stood there holding it. I wanted to throw it back in the pond and walk away but I couldn't.

In a small voice Merry said, "Well, this proves we aren't the only ones, doesn't it?"

Still holding the dripping skull at arm's length, I answered, "I think so . . . yes, this . . . person . . . has to be from a recent time. Cave people didn't have fillings in their teeth."

"No, probably not." Merry gave a small laugh. "Who do you suppose . . ." She shrugged and shook her head slowly. She was still gripping my arm.

The pancakes were holding steady so I breathed deeply and said, "There's no way we can find out that I know of but I think this . . . this fellow . . . has been here for a while . . ." I peered at the skull. "I wonder if the rest of him . . ." And I began to search the mud.

"Please, Chris, don't do that!"

"I have to, Merry. I have to . . . to . . ." And I pulled what looked like two leg bones from the mud. Now both my hands were full.

With a huge sigh Merry reached out and I handed her the skull and the other bones. She laid them on the bank then turned back to me. "May as well give me the rest."

I squatted and searched the mud. There were lots of bones. Neither of us is a anatomist so it wasn't until I found the second skull that we knew we had found two people.

Merry laid out the bones the way she thought they belonged in a human body and soon we had two almost complete skeletons laid out side by side. After a little rearranging here and there we decided that the bones belonged to adults and that one was about my height and the other as tall as Merry. Were they men? Two women? A man and a woman? We couldn't tell.

I had finally managed to resettle the pancakes. "What do you think we should do now, Merry?"

After a moment she said, "Bury them?"

"Bury them?" I echoed.

"Well, honey, I can't think of anything else, can you? We don't have any reason to keep them, do we?" Her face was anxious.

"Of course not. At least I don't think we do. We'll, ah, scoop out a hole in the mud and put them in it, okay?"

Merry nodded and gave me a tiny smile. So we began digging with our hands in the same place we'd found the bones. When we had the hole as deep as we thought it needed to be we couldn't decide which part to put in first. The hole was slowly filling with water and the sides were beginning to slump so we placed the longest bones in the bottom of the hole and then put the smaller ones on top and the skulls on top of that. We had not found the lower jaw of the first skull and there were probably some other parts missing but we did the best we could.

After we had finished we scraped mud until the hole was full and there was no sign that anything had been buried. The water seeped back and soon only the little cup-like depressions of our footprints showed that there had ever been anything at all.

We held hands and walked back the way we'd come. There were a million things going through my mind and I knew Merry was affected the same way because she wasn't saying anything either.

We reached our log and I rinsed my feet and sat to put on my boots. I gathered my weapons and Merry picked up the baskets and the canteen. Still without a word, we started home.

Merry was the first to speak. "These two people and that baby came here the same way we did, Chris. But these two may have been here for years and died of old age or they may have died of starvation or cold . . . but I think it was . . . well, they were there together so probably they died there at the same time . . ."

"You're thinking something killed them, aren't you?" I asked.

"Isn't that the way it looks to you? Either they died at the same time or were . . . killed . . . at the same time."

I thought about that for a moment. Finally I had to say, "I honestly don't know, Merry. I guess a hundred things could have happened and there's no way we can tell. We can't even guess, hon."

We walked a little farther. Merry said, "We'll get some more bait and come back in a few days, all right? I just couldn't eat crawfish right now."

I knew she meant that the two people had probably been eaten clean by the same kind of things that ate our bait and it was a little more than she could handle this soon.

We found Aroma snoozing under a tree. She jumped up and ran to Merry, grunting excitedly. Merry gave her a few absent-minded pats and we began filling baskets with fruit for the turkeys. Merry still didn't have much to say, but then neither did I.

It was a relief to reach our cave. Merry changed back into her shorts and I put my things away then went out and fed the turkeys some of the hard little balls we'd gathered for them. I knew that Merry and I would have to talk about what we'd found so that we could get it straight in our minds and then forget it. A picture of empty eye sockets and yellowed teeth kept floating through my head no matter how hard I tried to erase it.

Merry called me to lunch and I climbed the ramp. I wasn't hungry but I needed to be near her.

Lunch was sparse. Merry had boiled potatoes and smothered them in the meat gravy saved from supper. She had made a salad from green leaves that she'd left crisping in water this morning and sprinkled vinegar as a dressing. And there was tea.

"Chris, we need to talk," she said just as I forked the first bite into my mouth. "You're going to be all worried because you think I'm upset and I'm going to feel bad because you do, so we have to settle this thing."

I chewed and nodded. "Ummm," I answered.

"Good! Let me tell you what I think and you see if maybe you think I'm right." She sipped tea. "I think those people were here and died before we came. If they had been alive recently they'd have seen our fire on the cliff and we'd have ... met them. But at least they were alive in the last few years because of the fillings in their teeth. So we know that means other people have come here like we did . . ." She looked at me for support.

I swallowed a mouthful; I must have been hungry after all. "Yes, I think that's right."

"We haven't found any sign of a camp or a shelter of any kind around here and you've been all over for miles, haven't you?"

"Yes." I speared a tiny chunk of meat in the gravy.

"So, if they were found this close they probably lived near here and if we haven't seen where they lived that means weather and time have destroyed all traces, right?" She didn't wait for my answer. "I think that proves they weren't killed very recently. Or," she added, "that they didn't die recently, of whatever cause."

So far everything she said I had already thought.

"Now, we really can't know why they died but I think they weren't capable of caring for themselves like we are and probably died of hunger or exposure. They could have landed here in the dead of winter, you know." She sipped more tea.

"Agreed." I said. "The bones didn't look chewed or gnawed like they'd have been if something had eaten on them." I knew this was true because I had looked carefully without letting Merry know what I was looking for.

Now she was smiling, "So we don't have to worry about some huge animal."

"No," I said.

"And we don't have to worry about the same thing happening to us because we can take care of ourselves in winter or in summer or whenever."

"Yes," I said, nodding for emphasis.

"If you're through, how about finishing that little table you started yesterday."

And on that up-beat note I left for my chores after first kissing my Merry on the top of her head.

That evening after supper, we sat in our doorway and watched the sky darken, sipping hot tea. I was content that we had gotten through what could have been a seriously depressing situation. I had also finished the table Merry wanted. All of the little legs may not have been the same length but our floor wouldn't notice.

I heard Merry sigh.

"Honey, are you still sad?"

"I feel so sorry for them, Chris."

"I do too." And I really did.

"Can we go to bed now?"

I stood and cupped her face in my hands. "Yes," I told her, "and I'll hold you and keep you safe."

"I'd like that."

So, early as it was, we washed, brushed our teeth, banked the fire for the night, closed our door and got into our bed.

Merry huddled against me as I pulled the cover up over her shoulders and I held her, gently patting and stroking her back. I kissed her hair. "Please be happy, Merry. I love you so."

She moved closer and I tightened my arms around her softness. "I'll always keep you safe, darling. Nothing bad will ever happen to you because I won't let it."

I kissed her face, embracing all of her, trying to cover her with my love. "How can I ever tell you how much I love you? There aren't enough words . . ." I kissed her mouth. I would always keep her safe in my arms, I needed her to know that my lover was stronger than any adversity.

I kissed her again. "Darling, do you know how much, how very much I love you?" This was more of a declaration than a question. "I'll keep you safe for ever and ever . . . I'll hold you and keep you safe so nothing bad can ever touch you . . ."

I was aware, during my impassioned outburst, that she had moved my hand from her face and now held it captive between her legs.

I moved my fingers experimentally.

"Merry, you're so wet!"

"I think," she said wryly, "that I am sexually aroused."

"Really, darling, I wasn't trying . . ."

"Of course you weren't."

"Honestly, Merry, I wouldn't . . ."

"Of course you wouldn't. Now, my sweet baby, will you hush talking and get on with it!"

I would and I did.

Chapter XVI

I was feeling pretty smart, what with bringing home something almost every time I went to hunt or collect from my traps. If I didn't find meat, I'd see some growing thing I recognized or a plant we hadn't tried. At these times it seemed that we were simply playing at being pioneers; voluntarily trying our hand at self-sufficiency. This euphoria usually did not last long. The Damoclean sword of winter was constantly overhead.

We were both aware that our only staple through those three or four months would be smoked meat and fish and we knew that we needed green things if we wanted to keep from getting sick. We were feeling fine, hardly ever actually hungry although we did dream of the finer things in life like bread, for instance. The honey, which we had in abundance, helped our craving for sweets but sometimes I wanted ice cream so much I could taste it. Ice cream and butter and bread would have topped my list, with milk and coffee and ice for the tea way up in line. I still found myself reaching for a cigarette. Going cold turkey had been difficult.

"Chocolate for me," Merry said, "and tomatoes. Huge red tomatoes in a salad loaded with creamy cheese dressing. Also, ripe peaches would be nice."

There wasn't anything we could do about our longing for music but we did have our precious field guides for reading. And we did have options as far as food was concerned. Options within our limited range, that is.

At first I started each hunt with a feeling of excitement, not knowing what kind of thing I'd encounter, whether it would be big enough to eat me before I could kill it for us to eat. Now, however, I knew what to expect in the way of animal life.

The largest animal had been the deer and only that one. Many times I'd heard what sounded like a number of animals moving at the same time but my own inability to creep silently through the woods may have accounted in some way for the fact that I didn't encounter any herds. Even at my silent best, I probably made as much noise as ten elephants.

Most of the time, now, Merry and I went hunting together. We didn't like to be apart, especially after finding the two people in the swamp, so we'd usually pack a picnic lunch and follow the stream because that's where I had my traps hidden, on little trails that led to the water.

Merry was busy these days trying to make a jar with a cover that was airtight so we could store cooked greens. What she had made so far was good but it leaked water so we knew it wasn't tight enough and we believed it had to be. Merry thought the wax from the beehive would make a tight seal and she was experimenting with it.

She was also busy with the clay and the kiln so I had been walking my trap line alone. I was never too far from her, as the crow flies, and wasn't gone more than an hour or two at the longest.

Always, however, I was armed with my knife, the slingshot, my bag of rocks, the spear and the hatchet.

One morning, as I started out, my tennis shoes actually fell off my feet. I went back inside and put on my hiking boots. I was accustomed to going barefoot if the ground wasn't too rough but not when I walked my traps. As I was tying on my boots, Merry kissed me and told me not to be gone too long, then she went out to the kiln.

If I had known what kind of day it was going to be, I wouldn't have gone at all. But this is why Merry calls me the luckiest one and maybe she's right. I waved at her and Aroma from the stream bank and then I followed the curve of the stream towards my traps.

My first two traps, which I thought had been cleverly concealed, looked as if they'd been deliberately vandalized. The braided line which secured them to a stub pounded into the ground had been bitten in two, and the traps moved many feet from where I had set them and almost crushed by some heavy weight.

I felt the hair rise on the back of my neck. Something ugly had been at my traps, some huge creature I'd not seen before. I couldn't reset them; the doors were torn off. So I wound the line and hung it on a limb and then made my way cautiously to the next one.

The ground around this trap looked as if an army had held maneuvers there. Some of the holes were a foot deep.

I was really puzzled now. And scared. I stood very still and listened. Nothing.

Again I salvaged the line from the trap and then headed for the next one. I was about halfway there when I heard something coming through the brush behind me, something snorting and coming fast.

I'm not proud of my next action but it probably saved my life. I dropped my spear, grabbed for a tree limb, hoisted myself up and then climbed higher as fast as I could. From my safe vantage point I looked down and my mouth actually dropped open at what I saw.

A monstrous boar with tusks two feet long and weighing at least a thousand pounds came to a sliding halt under my tree and looked up at me with hateful red eyes. He was snorting and pawing the ground and making an awful racket. He ran around and around the tree so I climbed a little higher, being very careful not to lose my grip.

We stared at each other for a while but it was a Mexican standoff. I owned the tree and he owned the ground beneath it and neither of us would give an inch. I yelled at him, broke off branches and threw them down on him, cursed and cajoled but he stayed beneath the tree. A couple of times he stood on his hind legs and pawed at the trunk with his front feet. He was determined to get me.

Here I was, the mighty hunter, treed by a pig.

I thought about Aroma who surely was of a different breed than this monster. If she ever showed any disposition towards acting like this beast, I'd put her in the pot for sure. If I ever got back, that is.

Half an hour passed and I was getting more scared with each passing second. I knew Merry would wonder what happened to me and come looking. She'd walk right into the thick of it and that damned thing would kill her before she knew what happened.

So, more worried about Merry than I was about myself, I decided that it was time to go on the attack.

My spear was on the ground where I had dropped it but I still had the knife, the hatchet, my slingshot and a full bag of rocks. I tried the slingshot first. The tree was filled with prickly hard nuts we had not been able to eat because of the bitter taste. After I ran out of rocks I began using the nuts. I aimed at his head and snout and his eyes and was on target more than not.

He became annoyed.

I kept pelting him until I had to climb higher and reach farther for the ammunition. He was a little more than annoyed now. One eye was bleeding and he began shaking his head, white foam flying from his mouth.

Encouraged, I kept it up. Now he was really mad and he pawed the ground and ran around and around the tree. He was easier to hit when he stayed in one place but I was still scoring every other shot. Even so, I saw that he was ahead because I was still in the tree and it didn't look likely that I'd be down any time soon.

I thought about throwing the hatchet the way I'd seen it done in the movies but if I missed I'd lose the hatchet and he wouldn't have been slowed down at all.

I was almost out of reachable nuts so I figured that even if I didn't split his head open, which looked impossible to do anyway, maybe the blade would hit him deep enough so he'd bleed to death. Anyway, the hatchet wasn't doing me any good in my belt.

I waited for a while until he flopped to the ground, grunting and slobbering, and then I moved down the tree, moving slowly and making very sure of my grip. When I got to the lowest limb that I felt was safe I balanced myself on it, raised the hatchet over my head with both hands and threw it straight down at him as hard as I could.

The blade hit him just behind his head, in the fat part of his neck and buried itself almost out of sight. He stood up, shook his head violently from side to side, throwing the hatchet at least thirty feet, then turned and snorted off into the brush.

I stayed in the tree, listening to him until he was so far away I couldn't hear a sound. I added another ten minutes or so just to make sure, then I climbed out of the tree, collected my hatchet and spear, and started home at a fast trot. I was so glad to be alive!

Merry was still working at her kiln, doing something to the fire. She didn't look up when I slid to a stop, breathless and trembling.

"Hi, sweetheart," she said absently, "you back already?"

* * * * *

After I told and retold my story, adding details as I remembered them, Merry was very solemn. "We will never, not ever, go anyplace alone, do you hear me?"

"Yes," I agreed.

"Not even to the top of the cliff, not anyplace!"

I agreed to that, too.

Some days later, using our noses, we found the boar, dead. I hoped with all my heart that he was the only one of his kind around.

I did get plenty of TLC because of my adventure. My regret was that I didn't kill him on the spot so that we could have had smoked ham and fresh bacon and, perhaps, fat to make soap. Merry said she'd rather have me, safe and unhurt, than all the ham or bacon or soap in the world. Aroma, fatter than ever, rolled her eyes at this.

She was a fast growing pig and had almost doubled her size in the two months since we'd found her. I loved to grin at her and go "Yum, yum!" while making lip-smacking noises. She would run squealing to Merry, sure of protection and usually some tidbit and she would peer at me from between Merry's ankles, rolling her tiny eyes as if in terror. I think this was a game she played, knowing that I meant her no harm.

The cattails, which we collected frequently, were a welcome addition to our diet. The roots are sweet and delicious whether raw or roasted in the coals. Young shoots taste like cucumbers and we ate them raw, or boiled very briefly to bring back tenderness. We particularly enjoyed the white, delicate insides of the young stems. Either raw or cooked, they tasted like asparagus and had almost the same texture. Now that it was fall the flower spikes were loaded with pollen and we gathered all that we could to boil and eat like ears of corn. What we didn't eat I used to make baskets and mats. Merry decorated with them and Aroma consumed what little was left.

In between doing everything else there was always the sweaty, back-breaking labor of gathering the right kind of wood for our smoke house. We were pleased that our collection of smoked meat and fish was growing. Though unsightly, shriveled and black as pitch, each piece was beautiful to us.

We still caught fish by sneaking up on them as they sheltered behind the rocks but we used springs from the VW seats instead of the sheet as our net. We had deepened the hole and would catch fifteen or twenty in a short afternoon. It wasn't hard work, sitting quietly on the bank, the three of us, waiting for the water to calm and fish to collect in the hole. Very small ones we gave to Aroma. She learned not to approach the ones flopping on the ground until we had sorted them for size.

"See, I told you she was smart," Merry would praise her.

When we first brought Aroma home the turkeys were understandably worried that her voracious appetite would cause her to consider them as food but eventually they learned to accept each other. Aroma was short-tempered with them, however, and they kept a cautious distance.

When the fishing was done we would swim in the larger, deeper part of the stream. It was a chore to keep our water jugs full, so our swims were both for fun and for cleanliness.

We swam nude, of course, with Aroma watching from the bank. To tease, we'd splash her and she'd move just far enough away that the water couldn't reach her and not an inch more. Then she would lie there, her chin on the ground, very bored with our antics. We, however, were not bored. We would kiss underwater, testing who could hold her breath the longest. Or, we would kiss with our faces out of the water, our hands busy underwater. I liked to support Merry on one lifted knee, nibbling her breasts, laughing until we both sank.

What started as play soon became serious, the freedom of the water supporting us and giving an added dimension to our teasing. With Merry floating on her back, my shoulders supporting her legs, I kissed my way up the inside of her thighs. This was easier said than done, treading and swallowing water as I was. Merry's effort to keep her head above water and mine to keep us both afloat meant that I could not hold my position between her legs. So, her knees still hooked over my shoulders, I moved us to shallower water so that my feet were firmly touching bottom. Now that we were in less danger of drowning, I could concentrate on my own and Merry's pleasure.

She floated there, eyes closed, bottom lip caught between her teeth, legs open to me and my probing tongue. I lingered on those pink hills and valleys, for the time being ignoring the tiny mound of flesh that awaited my touch. Then Merry's choked, "PLease, baby!" told me to begin. I found the tiny swollen area and surrounded it with my lips, my tongue touching lightly. As I sucked, gently tickling, I could feel it harden and grow. Merry's legs locked around me and the slight thrusting of her hips as the tension mounted within her almost made me go under.

As she was about to come, Merry moaned. A sound like humming began deep in her throat. She was not aware of this, I know, because I'd asked her. I heard that sound now.

Her legs restricted the movement of my head but I had enough freedom to move slightly downward and slip into her. I loved her, the taste of her, the sweetness she gave to me as she gasped her pleasure. I waited, my tongue inside her, feeling the spasms abate, aware of her heat and the flowing moisture.

I supported her, her legs gradually relaxing and loosening their hold. I kept her head above water, moving her so that her head rested on my shoulder, my arms about her. I kissed what I could reach of her face and hair.

"Ah, Chris!" A long sigh, her breathing still rapid. She raised a hand to my face. "I love you, baby."

I tightened my arms around her, "I love you too, Merry. I love you too, my darling."

She raised her face for a sweet kiss, turning in my arms so that our breasts were touching. We kissed again, then again.

We were in very shallow water; we were, in fact, almost on the bank. "Do you want more?" I asked her.

"Yes,"she answered instantly, "but let me love you first."

Knowing how much making love to her had excited me, she moved me higher on the bank and knelt beside my legs. She touched me with her fingers, probing gently. My breath caught as she moved her hand. I felt her fingers in the slippery wetness.

"Oh, sweetheart, you're so ready!" And she touched with tiny circling movements, watching my face.

"Don't tease," I begged.

Merry smiled a secret, satisfied smile and bent as I opened myself to her.

I was so aroused that I came, almost instantly. It was so fast that I made almost no sound at all.

"If I didn't know you better I'd think you didn't enjoy that," she breathed, "but I do know you and I'll bet that you want more, too, don't you?"

"Ahhh . . ." I managed and her smile broadened.

"Well," she said, straddling my face, her own face between my legs, "let's do it together, shall we?"

The fish we caught were now stiff on the bank and Aroma was sleeping.

Why not?

Chapter XVII

It was near dark and the coals glowed cherry red, slowly cooking the main portion of our evening meal. My job was to see that the meat was done but not to the point of being blackened crisp, a job for which I was particularly unsuited. Looking into the spits of fire that hissed and turned to tiny towers of flame as the juices fell, I tended to daydream, often to the point of forgetting where I was and what my job was supposed to be.

There were so many things I wanted to do, too many things to accomplish in the few weeks I believed we had left before ice covered our valley. That it was fall was evident in the brilliant colors of the leaves of certain trees. The trees had been green when we came here seven months ago. We both supposed that here, too, leaves turned to yellow or red before they fell. And the leaves were falling. The afternoon winds made crisp little piles of them in corners and crevices and they crunched under foot on our well-worn pathways. A cold evening mist now drifted over the surrounding hills, a sure sign to my inexperienced eye that the winter I so much feared was almost upon us.

The meat, I decided, needed more cooking so I raised my gaze towards the distant mountains looking for . . . what?

The sun had set behind the mountains and our valley was now in darkness. I could not distinguish any feature of the landscape I knew so well. Even the tiny clear stream that we considered such a blessing reflected no light although I could hear it moving briskly toward the larger stream that crossed its path a mile or so to the south. There was no light in our valley. My fire was the only glow in darkness.

At first we had tried to light our area after dark so that there were no black corners and we could see each other, see light shining in the running water, light reflected back from the cliff walls, light everywhere.

Light was comforting and protected us from darkness, but the effort of supplying wood for all that fire left us exhausted, too tired to enjoy its flickering, fragile brightness. Whatever it was that was supposed to be afraid of fire and not attack, never even approached. Either the fire actually scared it away or it had never been there in the first place.

For my own peace of mind, I had chosen to believe that our valley was inhabited by us and by tiny creatures without ravenous tooth and claw. Time had not considerably altered my belief but time had changed me into a hunter of creatures, both large and small.

A hunter with a brain to devise clever weapons and traps is more than a match for any blundering animal, given favorable circumstances. Favorable circumstances had provided our supper now cooking slowly over glowing coals. We did not know, or care, what animal we were prepared to eat. That paleontologists would some day give it a long Latin name did not in any way affect our anticipation of an enjoyable feast.

The flesh was clean, slightly pinkish, very tender and quite delicious. In life the animal was the size of a large cat, short fur, rounded head, tiny ears and large forward-looking eyes. It made no sound that we had ever heard. It was particularly fond of fish, a fact of which I regularly took advantage.

A sound, as of someone moving quietly towards my back, caused me to smile.

"Who dat?" I asked.

Her laugh, soft, low, throaty, caused my breath to catch. At once I felt a hunger that had nothing to do with food.

"Can't sneak up on you, can I?"

"Good thing for both of us that I have ears like a hawk." I turned slightly. "Are you ready to eat, love? I think the meat is done enough."

"Smells delicious." She sniffed the air. "Should we eat here or go inside? I could bring the rest out, if you like."

"Inside, I think. It's getting cooler and this fire won't last too much longer." I leaned over and gingerly lifted the skewer from the supports.

"I wish I had some asbestos gloves so I could handle fire without getting burned."

Merry's laugh caused my skin to tingle. She touched my arm. "After supper," she promised, "we'll see how much heat you can handle."

Smiling — I am always pleased when Merry shows that she wants me — I walked carefully up the ramp and into our cave. Our wall sconces were burning brightly, lighting our cave with a soft glow and casting flickering shadows, an effect as pleasant as if we had planned it. The table was already set with a covered bowl of steaming yams, our own tender greens from the garden, and hot tea in our special cups. The silverware was assorted metal and clay but our dishes and cups, with their matching designs, looked elegant on palmetto mats. Merry took the skewer from me and served our plates, putting the remainder of the meat on a decorated platter, her newest addition to our pottery.

I enjoyed our supper time best of all. Knowing that we were through with work for the day, snug and warm, we could have a leisurely meal. Merry enjoyed this time, too. As we ate she'd tell me of her plans, wondering if it was possible for us to do some special thing she'd thought of. Even though I was always sure we had as many comforts as we were capable of making for ourselves, Merry could always think of something we still needed.

Often we sat long at the table, drinking more tea and talking about those things that lovers probably have always talked about. Tonight, however, remembering what Merry had said about my fire-handling abilities, as soon as I'd finished eating I sat on our log stool to kick off my thongs.

Before the second thong dropped, she was kneeling in front of me. Her eyes held mine as she reached up and began undoing the buttons of my shirt. "This," she said, concentrating on a button, "is how you start a fire."

She opened another button, then another, until my shirt fell open. "Stand up," she whispered, her hands on my hips.

Shakily, I stood.

Slowly she unzipped my jeans and pulled them down around my ankles. "Step out."

My heart now pounding furiously I eased the ragged denim off my bare feet and stood looking down at her upturned face.

She reached up and touched my breasts. I made a move to kneel. "No, stay where you are."

So I stood in the firelight, my shirt, much too large for me now, hanging loose from my shoulders and her hands moving slowly down my naked body.

"Now," she breathed, pulling my hips forward until I could feel the warm puffs of air as she spoke, "now we'll fan the flame." And her tongue made a wet trail from my navel down to the soft black fuzz.

I drew in a quick breath, my legs moving apart as her fingers touched, then opened me. I held her in place, my own fingers threading through her hair.

Her tongue found its way through the tangle of curls and I felt a gentle caress, a delicate touch that made my thigh muscles tremble. My knees began to give way.

So much I could endure and no more. "Merry, please," I managed to plead, "let me go to the bed!"

"Yes, baby, yes," she breathed, her voice thick. She rose from in front of me and, as we moved to our bed, she pulled off her shirt and stepped out of her jeans. I knelt to smooth the bed cover then lay on my back, knees far apart, and pulled her down to me. I lifted my hips so her tongue could begin touching me again.

Our lovemaking was usually deliciously long, passion building with each caress but tonight my need was instant and urgent. "Merry!" I moaned, my body shuddering. Her breathing, rapid and harsh, matched my own. I felt her tongue, stroking, stroking . . . then her fingers dug into my thighs and all feeling was suspended except that torrent of sensation which filled me and caused me to cry out.

For long moments I lay, relaxed, Merry's face resting on my thigh. "I love you, my darling," she murmured, her lips soft on my flesh.

So often, back in our own time, I had dreamed of loving Merry. After an evening at her apartment I would lie in my bed, sleep impossible, and imagine my hands moving beneath her clothing, feeling the smoothness of her thighs, the warmth and wetness as she opened herself to me. Then I would picture her naked, arms reaching to pull me to her, legs spread, eyes glazed with desire. Nothing I could have imagined was as sweet as the face I now saw above me, shadowed by the firelight.

"Are you all right, darling?"

"Yes," I breathed, desire again so strong I could hardly speak.

I pulled her face to mine. As we kissed I tasted myself; the odor of my sex on her lips and face. This so inflamed me that I had to take my mouth from hers in order to breathe.

I moaned Merry's name as I turned, cradling her head on my arm, my other hand cupping her soft breast then reaching to trace edges of the blonde triangle, fingers trembling. Slowly I dipped between her legs and drew my hand upward, pressing lightly. "Chris! Ahhh . . ." I repeated the movement, my touch firmer. This was excitement I could never have imagined; Merry's hips lifting as I stroked, her body straining to follow my hand.

Excited almost beyond control, I bent to find her breast with my tongue. I sucked, heart pounding, as Merry responded to the rhythm of my hand and mouth. Her breath caught and she moved convulsively, hips jerking as her knees spread wider. I was almost covering her body, her leg now captured between my own, and I pressed against that warm flesh as my fingers stroked and filled her.

I was aware of her rapid breathing and the low moan that started deep in her throat. I sucked harder as her hips strained upward. Then a long ragged breath. "Now," she pleaded, "Now!' And, for a timeless instant, the two of us moved as one. Then, relaxing, she closed her legs, trapping my hand in the wet softness. I kissed her, whispering of my love. Whispering of my need.

We made love again and again; loving gently, slowly, our kisses long and unhurried, climax a sweet release.

Much later, pressed close together, we lay on our straw mattress, smelling of sex, our hearts beginning to beat normally.

"Will it always be this way?" she asked, kissing my neck.

"What way?" I knew but I wanted to hear her say it.

"The way I get so ready when I think about you making love to me. If I think about what you do, I can even forget where we are. If I knew where we were, that is." She sighed a long, deep breath.

I tightened my arms about her. "I've heard that after a while lovemaking gets to be boring and people stop making love so much, or at least do it only once in a while."

"You've got to be kidding!"

"Nope. Sylvia said maybe it could get that way; but she changed partners so much she never got the chance to find out. I, personally, am not going to change partners and I'll bet I love you just as much in a thousand years as I do now."

"Do you think we're different from other people?"

"I know we are. Look at where we live and how we live. How many other people do you know who live in a cave?"

"Aroma?"

"She's not people. She thinks she's people but she's really not." I was very relaxed and sleepy. I shifted my shoulder under Merry's head and she snuggled closer, her arm across my waist.

"Are you going to sleep?"

"Probably. No, definitely. I am going to sleep." I pretended to snore and the last I remembered was Merry's soft lips on my cheek and her words, "I love you, baby."

Chapter XVIII

Contented and so very relaxed, we slept soundly until way past sunrise the next morning. Aroma, whose patience was long exhausted, nudged Merry's feet and grunted sourly.

"Time to get up, darling," Merry murmured somewhere near my ear.

"No, I'm not getting up today."

"Me either."

And we may not have except that Aroma pushed over her food basket and rolled it all the way across the floor to our bed and then onto the bed.

After Merry poured our first cup of tea she sat across the table and leaned towards me on both elbows. Her eyes still sleepy, she blinked and smiled. "We did make a night of it, didn't we?"

Trying to keep my eyes open too, I sipped the steaming liquid. "I think we set a record."

Merry's smile broadened. "Well, one of us set a record, I'll say that much."

I was still too sleepy to blush.

After breakfast I pulled on my boots and an extra shirt against the morning coolness and gathered my weapons.

"I'll be back soon. I haven't looked at the traps on the other side of the stream since day before yesterday and I don't like to leave things that long without food."

Probably we could have argued that it didn't make any difference because we were going to kill the animals anyway but I didn't believe in making them suffer for my laziness. So I walked down the ramp and turned upstream, walking with easy strides, now wide awake and feeling fine. I walked as far as the tree with my mark on it then moved into the underbrush where my trap was hidden.

This was going to be a good day! There were four bright eyes peering at me through the slats. I opened the trap over the basket and banged on the sides a few times, thinking to scare them into dropping out of one and into the other. They were resisting with both tooth and claw.

Merry had made a heavy mitten out of VW seat covering to use in this situation but I had forgotten to bring it and knew better than to grab at the little creatures with my bare hand — I had the scars to prove it.

The harder I banged the tighter they clung to the trap. Deciding that I needed a stick to poke at them, I turned away, taking a step for my hatchet. I never got to finish the step. The ground lurched under me and I fell hard to my knees.

EARTHQUAKE! my mind screamed as I scrambled to my feet, basket, trap and animals forgotten.

"MERRY!" I screamed aloud even though there was no hope of her hearing me.

My legs started moving towards the cliff even before I told them to. I couldn't tell if the earth was still shaking because I was moving so fast myself that I hardly touched ground. I ran along the stream bank, leaping over boulders, clearing obstructions as if I had wings.

It seemed to take forever but I finally came within sight of the fallen part of the cliff and our door opening. Merry wasn't at the kiln, I could see that as I flew past, she must still be inside! I found air and used it to yell her name, my legs still pumping, moving me towards the ramp. Then I saw her, coming out of the cave, Aroma trotting at her heels.

"MERRY!" I screamed, *"MERRY!"*

She started to run down the ramp but turned to look where I was. I watched, my feet pounding, breath rasping in my ears, as she lost her footing, fought for balance, failed and skidded off the edge of the ramp. Arms flailing, she fell, hit the sloping bottom edge then rolled down to the ground and lay still.

"NO!" I cried and I heard the echo in my head, *"NOoooooo!"*

My eyes on Merry's unmoving form, I tripped, fell, and plowed the ground with my face.

There is a distinct possibility that my legs didn't stop running because I have the impression that I covered many yards on my hands and knees, legs scrambling, until I was upright and headed towards Merry again.

Aroma and I reached her at the same time. I knelt by her body, so tiny and still, and gently, very gently, lifted her until my arms were snug around her, her head under my chin.

Aroma examined Merry's legs, sniffing delicately, then settled herself, head touching Merry's knee, her tiny eyes on Merry and then on me. We were frozen like that, the three of us. Quiet, except for the scream of denial that still filled my head.

I was not aware of any movement in the earth. But my heart was thudding so violently as it broke into a thousand jagged pieces that I would not have felt the cliff if it had crashed down on my head. I clung to Merry's body, my eyes squeezed shut, rocking back and forth, willing myself to die, too.

"Chris, I can't breathe."

Was this how death came? Did you hear the voice of your beloved as your own life waned?

"Chris, please, I can't breathe!"

I tightened my arms. I heard Merry's body groan.

"Merry? Merry?" I think I said those words. Then I flashed a picture of splintered ribs and crushed lungs and the noise inside my head cut off as if a switch had been turned. If this was a game that death was playing, I would keep up my part of the silly conversation until my breath stopped, too. So, as calmly as possible I said, "Where are you injured, Merry?"

"I'm not. You're squeezing me and I can't breathe."

I lifted my head from where it rested on hers. "Merry are you alive?"

"Yes."

I looked down at her. "You're not hurt?"

"No, just squeezed, not hurt."

My arms were trembling, I felt the strain. I relaxed them just a little. They began to shake uncontrollably.

"Merry . . . your head. It's all bloody. You *are* hurt!"

But you're alive, my mind was singing, *REALLY, REALLY ALIVE!*

"That's not my blood, Chris, it's yours."

"Mine?" I closed my eyes again.

"From your nose, I think, and you have a cut on your chin." Her voice was gentle and calm. Much too calm.

"You're sure it's mine?" My arms were going to fall off.

"Yes, it's . . . raining . . . down on my head."

"Raining?" I opened my eyes and looked at her head. I looked for a long time.

"Merry?"

"Yes, darling?" She lay very still.

"I think I'm going to be sick."

We moved apart just in time.

* * * * *

After I rinsed my mouth in the stream and Merry had washed her face, she looked at my chin.

"Maybe, maybe not," she said, turning my face to inspect the cut. "It's deep but not too long. Anyway, it's almost stopped bleeding . . . just oozing a little." She sat next to me. "Do you think you can walk to the cave, Chris?"

"Sure, why not? It's my chin that's cut, not my legs!"

"Honey, have you looked at your knees?"

I looked. More rips and tears in the faded denim and, to my astonishment, a few rips and tears in the skin, too.

"Merry, I had no idea!" I touched my knees and winced. "I was so worried about you being dead that I didn't even feel my knees!"

"You'll probably feel them even more by tomorrow." She stood and held her hand to me. "Get up, honey, let's find out if we still have a home."

Aroma following, we walked to our ramp. Everything looked the same so we walked up to the entranceway. No changes here that we could see. We moved cautiously down our hallway to the cave opening and, peering inside, saw that everything was in its accustomed place. The greens that Merry had been cooking for lunch were still simmering on the stove, plates undisturbed on the table. There did not appear to be any damage at all, none.

"It was an earthquake, wasn't it?" I had to ask because all I remembered was that one huge shift as the earth heaved. If there had been any quivering and shaking, as I imagined occurring during an earthquake, I had not felt it.

"I thought so," Merry answered. "There was a quick kind of bump that I mostly felt through my feet. It wasn't very, ah, distinct . . . more like something happening far away. I waited a few seconds and didn't feel anything else so I kind of shrugged it off." Merry frowned, reliving those moments. "It was when I heard you calling that I got frightened."

"If you were frightened, I was scared out of my skin! I had to get to you, don't you see!" And now, remembering my fear, my heart started pounding furiously. "I thought you were dead . . . you didn't move or say anything . . . " I covered my face with my hands, blacking out the memory.

Merry covered my hands with hers and gently pulled mine down. "Don't," she said softly. "Don't do that. You're making your chin bleed again."

* * * * *

"So," Merry said, as she carefully cleaned my face with the damp cloth, "it was just that the wind was knocked out of me when I fell. And I may be a little bruised here and there." She rinsed the cloth in clean water then squeezed it almost dry and began wiping again.

"How did you learn to fall that way? I'd have broken every bone in my body."

It wasn't all that easy to speak with a rag over my mouth but I was trying to keep Merry distracted by talking about anything and everything. Her hands had started to shake and her face was set, her teeth clenched. Reaction, I knew, from what had happened this morning.

"Oh, judo, I guess or . . . " Her voice trailed off then started again, "Or . . . I ski, you know, and in gym . . . " Now she stared at me, the cloth pressed to my cheek, and I watched her eyes fill with remembered terror, then saw tears begin to run until they dripped from her chin. We stared at each other. Then my arms, reaching, met hers and we held each other wordlessly.

* * * * *

We were sipping hot tea. Merry had washed her hair, my hair, had put our clothes to soak. We were clean and dry, and the horror of what might have been was fading. Not fading, however, were the terrible bruises on Merry's right side. They were getting darker and swelling and, I knew, more painful by the minute, but Merry wouldn't admit it. She was more concerned with me.

"I think your chin needs to be stitched, Chris, but I really hate to do it."

"I'd really hate to have you do it, too, so please don't." I could be very firm.

"No, we have to do something about that cut and I have an idea."

"If it involves sewing, forget it, all right? You have enough sewing to do on my jeans without worrying about my face." I hoped my determination showed.

With a calculating look in my direction, Merry went to the woodpile and began searching through the neatly piled logs.

"Merry?" She didn't answer. "Merry, are you going to club me so I won't feel it? That's kind of drastic, don't you think?"

"That's one way," Merry said, laughing, "but I think I've found another."

She brought a fresh cut piece of wood to the table. I watched her cut a tiny strip of cloth from her precious hoard of clean rags. "Come, sit here where there's light," she ordered. Curiosity high, I sat where she wanted and held up my chin for whatever she was going to do.

"This cut needs to be held together and we're both too chicken to do it the way it probably should be done so I'm going to hold it together." And she put a dab of sticky tree resin on each end of the tiny strip of cloth. "With this kind of butterfly Band-Aid." I felt her touch my chin and smelled the piney odor of tree sap as she glued the bandage to the skin on either side of the cut, closing the wound and covering it with clean cloth at the same time.

I wiggled my jaw. "Feels okay, Merry."

She touched my cheek. "I don't want you to be scarred like a boxer." Her smile was tender. "But, between the two of us, we're doing a pretty good job on your fact."

"Well," I said, "as long as this glued togetherness doesn't interfere with kissing . . . or other things . . . it'll be an acceptable substitute to sewing, I think."

To show me that the Band-Aid wasn't in the way of anything, Merry kissed me.

To show her that my chin was fine, Band-Aid and all, I returned her kiss.

* * * * *

Long after Merry had fallen asleep that night, I lay awake. Rain had begun late in the afternoon and was still pouring hard so I just listened and stared up into blackness, trying to ignore the dull, steady ache in my chin and the painful throb in both my knees.

Mostly I was trying to imagine the two of us building a wooden shelter somewhere in the open so that when the earth closed in on our cave we would have another place ready to move into. I tried making a list of the things we'd have to duplicate so that our shelter would be stocked, at least, with the bare essentials. By the time I reached the fourth or fifth item I had forgotten the first so, mentally exhausted, I'd go back and start over.

It was no use. I knew that we could build a lean-to sort of shelter, but at best it would only prolong our misery until we froze to death or until we starved. We were relatively snug in our cave; dry and warm and safe from wind and snow and freezing cold. We had a good chance of living through the winter if winter didn't last too long and if an earthquake didn't smash us flat. But out-of-doors, in a flimsy wooden shelter, we would not last any time at all.

I did not want to be here. I did not want to be in this place where the walls could close in on me and the ceiling drop on my head. I did not want to lie here, hurting. I was not in the least enchanted by the primitive life we were forced to lead. I wanted toothpaste and soap and ice cream and coffee. I wanted shoes and books. I wanted music and butter and warm gloves. I wanted to be safe in a world I knew how to handle.

"Do you want me to hold you, darling?" Merry's voice was soft and full of sleep.

I sighed. "Yes," I answered. "Yes, please."

Merry turned and carefully slid her arm under my neck. "Slip down a little and rest your head on my shoulder. Be careful of your chin, love."

I fitted my body to hers. And as I lay, listening to her soft breathing, everything suddenly became clear to me.

All I really wanted was Merry.

* * * * *

The next morning Merry's entire body was so stiff and painful that she needed my help just to sit up in bed. For the next few days one particular place on her side caused agony when she breathed and I believed that a rib was cracked or bruised, but Merry said it wasn't too bad and after a while it hurt only when she moved a certain way or took a deep breath. Massage, however, seemed to help her shoulder so I rubbed and kneaded morning and night. Merry said what made her shoulder feel best of all was me kissing it to make it well, a form of therapy we both enjoyed. Even so, it was weeks before she could move normally. The cut on my chin closed in a matter of days and healed without incident.

We must have been a pitiful sight for a while; me with my chin glued together and limping because my knees would neither bend nor straighten, and Merry, her right shoulder hunched, arm stiff and almost unmoving at her side, walking with slow, cautious steps and trying her best not to yawn.

Our "infirmities", as Merry called them, were not so serious in themselves but I lay awake many nights thinking "what if" . . . What if my chin had not healed . . . what if the cut had become infected? What if one of Merry's ribs had splintered and pierced a lung . . . or some vital organ? She could have cracked her skull, broken an arm, a leg . . . her neck!

These thoughts were not productive, and finally I managed to put them far enough back in my mind that they surfaced only once or twice during the day and at night, just before sleep, as I took a final look at the tons of ceiling hanging over our heads.

Chapter XIX

"Sweetheart, I need a vacation." Merry was slicing meat to make stew. She was barefooted, standing on the kitchen mat which I'd made from the palmettos that grew along the stream.

I didn't look up, my hands were busy working on another mat for our table. "Where would you like to go?" I asked. "Acapulco is nice in the summer. Or how about Niagara Falls? We could have a proper honeymoon . . . " I was beginning to warm to the subject.

The sound of rain, hard and driving, came clearly through our door. It did not drown out what was clearly a sniff from Merry. I looked up, surprised.

"Honey, are you crying?" Even though her back was to me I could tell she was. I dropped the mat and went to her, turning her to face me, seeing tears flowing freely from her beautiful eyes. I held her, wrapping her in my arms.

After a few minutes she lifted her face and a tiny, red-nosed smile told me the crying was done. I wiped her cheeks with my fingers.

We sat together on our sofa, Merry perched sideways so she could look at me. I reached for her hands and held them in mine.

She shook her head. "It's just so awful . . . " Her voice trailed off.

I knew what she felt. It had rained for days, a hard downpour with black skies and everything damp. It was late autumn and we had almost forgotten that the skies had once been blue. The rain was cold and the drops were huge. Merry had made a sort of bonnet for me out of parts from the VW rubber floor mat but it didn't keep my head dry, all it did was keep the rain from hitting my face directly when I hunched against the wet to walk my trap line.

Even the animals were holed up. My traps had yielded only one shivering, wet creature, the one Merry was preparing for our supper.

"Merry, are you sure it's only the weather? You're not sick or anything, are you?"

She shook her head again. "No, but I'm so tired of being here. There's nothing to do . . . I think I'm just bored." Seeing my look, she added, "Not bored with us, darling, just with . . . just with being so dark and so wet . . . " She stopped, sitting forlorn with one bare foot resting on the other, her hands cold in mine.

"Honey, why didn't you tell me you were feeling low?"

She answered instantly. "Because it makes you feel so bad when I feel bad that I hate to tell you."

I started to talk but she hushed me with her hand. "Chris, we're both trying to make the best of what is, to say the least, a very trying situation and sometimes one of us is bound to get a little low. It doesn't mean you're the cause of my feeling that way but you always think so, don't you darling/"

"Well, I guess so . . . probably."

"Where we are and how we have to live would make anybody's spirits droop once in a while. I think the only thing that keeps me sane is the fact that I love you so much!"

I sighed. "Sometimes I feel that way, too."

"I know you do. I can always tell because you pretend to be very busy so I won't see how you feel. Isn't that right?"

"I guess so."

"It works both ways, honey. I started thinking about my parents and how much I miss them . . . how sad they must be . . . and that made me sad, too. Then our garden washed away in all the rain . . . But I pretended everything was okay because I didn't want you to get upset. I think it's all right if we try to spare each other once in a while, don't you?"

Her logic was irrefutable, as usual. I asked, "You know what makes me sad sometimes? My cat. I wonder about my cat . . . if the cleaning lady remembered to feed her and if someone thought about her being there alone after we disappeared."

"Oh, Chris, you know Sylvia and Bessie remembered her. I'm sure they have her right now . . . and are spoiling her to death, too."

Comforted, until the next time I thought about it, I hugged my Merry and lightly kissed her sweet lips.

"Can't you do better than that?"

"Think so," I said and kissed her firmly on the mouth.

"Huh!" She was grudging. "Guess that's better than nothing!"

I had to laugh and I hugged her tighter. At that moment I would have given anything to be able to make the rain stop and the sun shine. I tried to think of what I could do to make Merry feel better and bring a real smile to her sad face.

Mentally, I went over a list of the activities available to us and decided that we had already done everything ten times over. We had played every card game we knew with our homemade deck. We played checkers. We moved the furniture around, then moved it back. Merry worked with clay and I wove mats and baskets and we both read and reread the field guides. We had tried to keep busy but, even with our moss and wood torches going full blast, the light was dim and the air was damp and we both had slight headaches most of the time.

We stayed late in bed. One or the other of us would crawl out of bed and build up the fire to make tea, then we'd snuggle together while we drank, often going back to sleep for a while. Since there was no morning sunlight to brighten our cave we were never sure of the time. Not that time, in the usual sense, had much meaning for us.

Except for the eggs we had pickled, our supply had been cut off when the baby birds started hatching, so our breakfast was often leftover supper. Merry served each meal, formally, at our table.

"We may live in a cave," she had informed me, "but we will remain civilized." So we stayed civilized even though the sky had fallen and continued to fall at an alarming rate.

I squeezed her hands. "When the rain stops we'll forget how bad it's been." She made a face at me, so I added, "It can't rain forever." I wasn't entirely sure of this but I wanted to reassure her. I couldn't stand seeing her so miserable.

It wasn't easy for me, either. I kept thinking about winter. If a week or so of rain could make us this unhappy, what was it going to be like when the time stretched to months?

Merry sighed. "If it's this bad now, hon, what's it going to be like if we're frozen solid in here this winter?"

I should have known that she had though about it, too. I said, "What did the cave people do all winter? They were in the same fix, you know."

"I don't think they thought about it one way or the other. I mean they didn't know any other life, they had no alternatives to think about. Probably they just ate and stared at the fire and . . . you know." She smiled at me.

Of course I knew what the other thing was that they did. The same thing we spent much of our own time doing.

Continuing the thought, Merry said, "If we're going to be stuck in here for months maybe we should think about what to do instead of just concentrating on what to eat and how to keep warm, don't you think?"

"Yes," I told her, "I think that's probably what I thought, too." At her look of approval, I added, "Uh . . . did you have anything specific in mind?"

"Well, for starters, you can teach me how to weave baskets and things. I'd like to see more color and different designs. Not," she added, "not that yours aren't lovely, just that I'd like to be able to dye the palmetto and the reeds like I did with some of the clay." She thought for a moment. "We could color-coordinate our pottery with our mats . . . that would certainly make time pass, wouldn't it?" She smiled with delight. "We'd have the only cave in the world with matching everything!"

Her face alight now, she explained to me how much better we'd feel if we worked on our decor. I watched her hands sketch patterns in the air and her eyes widen with pleasure as she described her ideas to me. I wanted to take her in my arms and hold her but I hadn't seen her this animated for days and I didn't want to interrupt the flow of inspiration. It made me feel a thousand times better to see my Merry happy again; better, yet saddened, too. How little it took, how simple her need that a few crushed berries could lift her spirits so.

"Darling, you're not listening to me!"

"Yes I am. I was just thinking about hauling plenty of palmetto fronds and reeds so we won't run out, that's all."

"Well, what do you think about the lights?"

"Um, what do I think about the lights?" I didn't think anything at all about the lights but I knew better than to say so.

"I know they'll work and I can't wait to try!"

"Will you, ah, explain it to me again, love, so I'm sure I understand." This seemed a safe thing to say.

"Chris! I knew you weren't listening! I could tell by your expression."

I grinned at her. "I'm listening now."

She looked exasperated but I knew she really wasn't. "What you're going to do," she began, "is cut some metal out of the car, about the size of a sheet of legal paper and we're going to scour one side with sand from the stream bottom to make the metal shine. Then we'll bend it in a U shape and put it behind the torches. That way we'll have reflected light, much brighter than a torch alone! Why, we may put reflectors behind all our torches and make this place light up like Broadway!"

I liked the idea. It would be wonderful to have enough light to read in the evenings. Our sleeping habits had changed since the camping trip. Now we usually went to bed when it got dark and got up with the sun. But we weren't always ready for bed when the sun went behind the mountains so more light would be a blessing.

"Merry, that's the best idea since the wheel. Soon as the rain stops I'll chop some metal for you."

Cheered by this and the other plans she was making, Merry went back to her supper preparations and I picked up my mat and we went on about our evening. I was glad that she could cry out some of her frustrations and almost wished that I could have done the same.

Later, Merry was washing dishes when she turned to me, "Chris, do you smell anything?"

Before supper I had noticed a faint electric kind of odor in the air but now it was very strong. I knew what the smell meant. Because of the downpour being so noisy and the thunder already so constant, we hadn't noticed anything different.

I went to the door and peered out, seeing long flashes of lightning on the mountain slopes. They were a good distance away but it seemed that each flash was closer and brighter than the one before.

Merry had followed me and stood, leaning against me, peering out the glass. "It's that time again, isn't it?"

"Yep, guess so. Shall we watch?"

"Of course, love. I'll get more tea and we'll open the door. Will you get stools so we can be comfortable?"

So, each wearing two shirts because of the evening chill and the dampness, we sat in our hallway sipping hot tea and watching the lightning. It was a regular occurrence and always a spectacular display but had never been quite as bright and noisy as the night of our camping trip.

Sometimes the lightning came to us and other times it seemed to spend its fury in some other place. There were at least six spots in the valley that seemed to attract it but our area seemed to be the favorite and we smelled the strange odor only when it was headed our way.

This evening, eventually, the bolts made their way to us and flashed to the ground just outside our cave. Tonight the color fizzled without particular brightness and we could watch it with our eyes wide open. The sound was loud but we were accustomed to it now and we would clap and cheer at the brightest bolts as they danced along the ground. It was like having our personal fireworks display and we enjoyed every minute.

After thirty minutes or so, when it was over, we brought our stools back inside and closed our door.

Following our usual pattern, I washed first and got into bed. Merry then heated her water and I watched as she cleaned herself and brushed her teeth. These were always special moments for me, watching her move in the firelight, turning this way and that, bending, stretching.

I wanted to touch her. I needed to feel her softness.

"Hurry!"

She looked at me and smiled. "Yes, baby, I'm coming."

As I lay there, waiting for her to come to me, the rain stopped.

Chapter XX

Months ago we had both agreed that we were living in a prehistoric valley, that the strange foliage growing all over the place, some of which we identified from the fossil book, was native to the valley and actually belonged where it was—but the things that were familiar to us, some trees and plants and birds and our turkeys, to name a few, had been brought here by lightning the same as we had been. This was a frightening presumption but the facts, as we saw them, led to this conclusion.

"We should thank the lightning for not landing us in the middle of the Cretaceous period," Merry said as she leafed through the fossil book for the thousandth time. "The animals there were ferocious and very plentiful. I think I like it better where we are."

"Me too, Merry." I had almost memorized the fossil book by this time and I thanked the lightning for this large favor. "It's good we're in a peaceful place. Think if we had to duck dinosaurs all day!" I shivered at the thought.

"I'm sure you'd handle it some way, sweetie." Merry was more confident of my abilities than I was.

"Well, I remember movies where people were living at the same time as some of those monstrous creatures and somebody in the tribe would always outsmart the dinosaur." I laughed. "Those animals did have little heads for so much body, didn't they? Probably wasn't hard to out-figure them." I was trying to reassure myself in the event that I had to out-think a thirty ton brontosaurus. Not too likely, but I wanted to believe that I had an edge.

"Speaking of movies, honey, what about those that dealt with time? Do you remember how people moved back and forth in funny looking machines?"

I stopped chopping and wiped my face on the towel that Merry had brought with her. "No, not really." I threw the towel back to her and started chopping again.

Merry stood to hang the towel on a low limb. Even though I knew every inch of her body, I still enjoyed watching her move. Her clothes were threadbare now, as were my own, and I could see those lovely round nipples, dark under the faded yellow shirt.

"Well, if you go back in time and change anything then the future you came from would be changed in some way. At least that's how I remember it."

"So when you got back to your own time you would be the same but everything else would be changed?"

"Uh huh. so when we kill animals to eat, we could be changing the future in some way. Or birds or even turtles."

I had been chopping furiously, making small logs out of big logs. "I guess that could happen, Merry, but we haven't any way of knowing if it's taking place. I really wouldn't like to think that my supper made it possible for, say, Hitler to win the way."

Merry idly scratched Aroma's ears, much to Aroma's delight. "Think of this, darling. What if things are so changed in the future as a result of our actions in this time that we don't meet at Sylvia's party."

Time to sharpen the hatchet. I sat on the log next to Merry and took out the sharpening stone. It was mostly worn away so I used it carefully. "I guess what you just said didn't happen because we are here in this time as a result of meeting in a future time, aren't we?"

Merry was gleeful. We hadn't run out of things to talk about but this was a new twist to the subject. "I think," she began, "that this valley is sort of special. Look around you, hon, at the mountains and how tall they are."

Obediently I swiveled my head. Merry was right, of course. We were ringed by mountains and they were very tall. Most days the clouds were streaming far below the ragged peaks.

"Can you imagine anything getting over those mountains? Except a plane, of course."

I shook my head, admitting that I couldn't imagine what she said.

"Well, whatever is here in this valley would stay here in this valley, wouldn't it? And things on the outside stay on the outside?"

I nodded, aware of what was coming next.

"Doesn't that suggest anything to you?"

I shook my head, even though I did have an inkling. In fact, what Merry was saying crystalized some thoughts I had from way back, even though I had not verbalized them.

"This valley is a dead end, sweetie, nothing new gets in and nothing from here gets out. Except for what the lightning brings, that is. So, whatever lives and dies here doesn't change the future or the past and probably doesn't make any difference to the present, either."

"You're right, of course. We haven't seen any dinosaurs because there aren't any and Aroma is probably a modern pig." At this Aroma snorted softly before shifting her position against Merry's leg. "And our turkeys as well, and the other things, trees and such. But I'll bet on the other side of the mountains we'd find every one of those damn big animals."

"Probably, probably." Merry stood and reached for the towel. "Let's go home now, I want to check our dinner. There's a possibility my new crock pot has fallen apart. Remember the last one? That'll mean no supper."

I was picking up wood, making a small armload for Merry and a generous one for me. "Merry, do you think we should make a cart for Aroma to pull? She eats as much as we do, she ought to contribute something." And I stuck out my tongue at Aroma as she passed me trotting towards home.

Merry added a couple of pieces to her armload. "Honey, I'm really stronger than you think. I can carry as much as you."

"I don't want you to have to."

We walked for a few minutes. "Chris, what you just said gave me an idea."

"What did I just say?" I knew what I just said.

"About a cart. Honey, do you think you could?"

Chapter XXI

We were so tired. All day we had been collecting wood in piles, a long line of piles stretching at least a mile into the forest.

Our usual method of wandering with an armload, picking up pieces as we walked, was not efficient. Plus we didn't get much wood. Now we walked away from our cliff in a straight line, making piles of usable wood as we went. Then we walked back, stopped at the first pile, bundled as much of it as we could with our rope and both of us pulling, dragged it back to the ramp. Usually we had made the bundle bigger than we could haul up to the cave even though the incline was not very steep.

We hauled wood all day to stack inside our cave. Stacking and sorting and chopping was as tiresome as hauling but we knew that our lives might depend on the amount of wood we had collected so we kept desperately at it.

A sudden drop in temperature had frightened us. The mist, like a heavy fog, hung in the air until well past mid-morning and began collecting again before the sun was down. I saw the fear in Merry's eyes. She tried to hide it behind a cheerful smile but her dear face was so known to me that I could read her thoughts.

The nights had become uncomfortably cold and only the two sleeping-bag coats Merry had made for us enabled us to be up and out before the sun had burned away the damp. We were very snug in our down-filled coats but we didn't think that they would be enough to keep us warm in the outdoors once real winter set in.

In our minds was the knowledge that we would be forced to stay in the cave when the snow grew deep, our lives depending on what we had collected and stored. Neither of us could accurately estimate the amount of food necessary to keep us and Aroma and the turkeys alive through a winter, the length and severity of which we could not guess.

Our new metal stove was a delight and kept the room quite comfortable so that we could eat and bathe and then spend time reading. Merry's idea about the VW metal reflecting light was nothing short of genius. We could now read without causing the dull headaches that had so bothered us before. Some evenings were spent talking or just watching the fire burn down before slipping under our remaining coverlet. Thank goodness for sleeping bags and the fact that we had two of them.

Tonight we were both exhausted. Merry dozed restlessly and turned often, trying to find a comfortable position. As tired as I was, I had not been able to sleep. I shifted too, but sleep wouldn't come. Finally, Merry snug against my side, I drifted.

A crash of lightning, like the toll of doom, awakened both of us in an instant. The sound was so violent the floor shook and we sprang upright, reaching for each other. Through the tiny glass in the door our cave was lighted with a white hot glow, too bright for our eyes. We both knew what was happening but were not ready for the violence and the earth-shaking sounds.

"Oh, my God!" Merry cried, covering her ears and burying her face on my shoulder. I held her close against me, my own eyes squeezed shut against the terrible light. I was so thankful that it was the lightning and not another earthquake.

We had been awakened like this a month before; the thunder and the lightning and the ground shaking and the smell of electricity in the air. That time, too, we clutched each other, trembling in mortal fear. Our friendly lightning was now like hell unleashed, the same fury as the night of our camping trip. The unbearable noise and the flashes of fiery light continued for half an hour. Before it ended, realizing again that we weren't injured, only frightened, we had walked to the door and looked out through the glass.

All of the activity was in the same place as usual — the area measuring not more than fifty feet in diameter. The VW was sitting directly in the center of an indescribably bright glow.

As the light dimmed enough what we could see through lids squeezed almost shut, we saw three figures, three human figures, standing in the air just above the little car. One raised an arm and pointed directly at us, as we cowered behind our flimsy door. The other two turned and peered in our direction but there were no distinct features that we could see. As we gaped, the figures dimmed and disappeared. We stood staring as the lightning moved away and the thunder became just a soft rumble in the distance.

I had piled wood on the fire and Merry calmed Aroma who had been hiding under our straw bedding. We both stood at our stove watching water heat for the tea that would help calm our nerves. We needed to make sense out of what we had seen because neither of us could believe what our eyes had shown us.

I suggested to Merry that we had been hallucinating and she said with a sniff that two sober people didn't hallucinate the same thing at the same time. On this stalemate we had returned to bed, lying sleepless for a long time.

But tonight, one month later, now that the initial shock had worn off somewhat we threw back the cover and ran to the door. Because of the brightness we stood, Aroma huddled at our feet, waiting for the light to dim.

As we peeped through the glass triangle, we could see that the VW was glowing, every part of it bathed in a white light, as if the metal skeleton was lighted from within. Then the light seemed to dim and the VW disappeared. It simply ceased to exist. It was there and then it wasn't.

We kept watching but soon the lightning was gone, and with it the light. We could see only blackness outside our door.

We made tea, laced generously with honey, and sat on our sofa, the coverlet wrapped around us. We asked each other what this meant. Each of us answered the other with a shrug. Finally we went back to bed.

As soon as the first morning light appeared, we bundled up in our coats and went outside. There wasn't even a scorch mark on the ground. The car was gone, as cleanly as if it had never been and my only pair of pliers with it.

We kept hauling wood. Finally, while on a break, we sat in the woods talking. We agreed that the lightning was a time-warp display. Actually, Merry made that decision and I simply agreed with her. She had read of time warps in the science fiction stories she liked so much and this, she said authoritatively, met the criteria. Although she couldn't explain what a time warp actually was, she said that generally it was something that picked up things in one time and carried them to another. At this very scientific explanation, I nodded.

"So now the VW is resting on its rims in some other time?" I asked.

"Probably. In some past time, or," she added lamely, "or in some time or other ..."

I wanted better than that. "What about the people we saw drifting in the air?"

Merry thought for a moment, then smiled at me. With an airy wave of her hand she said, "They were from a time in the future, come to invite us to a party. We could have gone, too, except we don't have the right clothes." Now she was laughing loudly.

I had to laugh, too. I had a mental picture of us showing up at the door in our clean but ragged shirts and jeans, patched all over, hiking boots scuffed and worn, with our bed-roll coats thrown casually over a shoulder. We were both in tears, laughing hysterically, Aroma grunting and squealing and trying to hide under Merry.

After a day or two, we began to accept the Time Warp theory. Why not? We certainly didn't have a better explanation. Anyway, this fit our original thinking of the lightning as the transfer mechanism. Also, it gave us a name for what happened when the lightning did its thing.

Although I had scavenged from the VW virtually everything usable, I missed it. It had been our constant reminder of home, a link with our past. I wasn't sure how

Merry felt until she commented that since the VW really wasn't useful anymore, she was glad to have it gone. "We looked like trash with that rusting derelict in our front yard." So, that was that.

Our experience with the "display," as we called it, had sobered both of us. We knew that it wasn't part of a dream, that things actually came and went when the lightning flashed in that particular way in that certain place and we felt that the place where the VW had been, the place where we had landed, was a sort of platform where the exchanges took place. Where the things came from or where they disappeared to, we couldn't even speculate. So we speculated endlessly.

We were sure of one fact, however. Winter was close. We could see our breath hanging heavy in the October air and the trees were almost bare.

We kept hauling wood until every nook and cranny of our cave was piled high. Having no gloves was a considerable hardship and so we wrapped our hands with rags, even though we had few of them, to protect our freezing fingers from the roughness of the wood and the chilling cold.

Our sleep was uneasy now in spite of the comfort provided by walls full of wood and more wood stacked at the bottom of the incline. Even the racks of smoked fish and meat, the jars of honey and pickled greens and the baskets of nuts, dried berries, potatoes, onions and yams were somehow only slightly reassuring.

Our routine was much the same as always, except that it got colder. We now did all of our bathing in the cave, hauling water from the stream to fill our jugs and to heat on the stove. Our stream ran ice water now, too cold for bathing even in the middle of the day.

Merry went about her tasks, cheerful as always, smiling at me when our glance met, touching me when we were close, holding me in the night, loving me frequently.

One night as we lay together, almost dizzy from the intensity of our lovemaking, she whispered in my ear, "Do we make love so often because we love each other or because there's nothing else to do?"

I was basking in the glow of sexual satisfaction, my body satisfied, every muscle relaxed and limp. Her words penetrated the fuzziness between my ears. "Huh, what did you say?"

"You heard me. Which is it?"

"Well," I stuttered, "because we love each other, of course."

She was leaning over me now, insistent. "But if we were back home would we spend so much time in bed?"

"Even more, my love!" I wrapped her tighter in my arms, throwing a leg over her hips.

"How come more? Tell me!"

I forced myself to concentrate. "Because we would be more comfortable and we could bounce around. You have to admit this straw isn't the softest mattress you've ever had!"

Merry was silent for a long minute. Then she said, "I'm glad it's from love and not from boredom. You know, sweetie, if it was because of nothing else to do, I don't think either of us would be able to walk after a winter spent in this cave. There'd be nothing to do but eat and fuck and put wood on the fire; eat and fuck and put wood . . ."

I covered her mouth with my hand.

* * * * *

She could always think of the darnedest things to ask me. We were sitting at the table after supper, the fire roaring in our stoves, sipping our honey sweetened, lemon flavored tea.

"When we make love, which of us is the man?"

"What do you mean, which of us is the man?"

"That's what I mean, what I said. Which one of us is the man?"

I put my cup down on its matching saucer and stared at her.

She widened her eyes. "Don't look at me like that. Answer my question!"

"Okay . . . the answer is . . . neither of us!"

"You mean when I'm doing all those things to you, I'm not the man?"

"Why do you have to be a man? Can't we just be two women? When I'm making love to *you* do you think of me as a man?" I think my voice was getting louder.

"No," she answered, "I know you're a woman."

"And when you're making love to *me* I know *you're* a woman, too." My voice *was* getting louder.

"You don't have to raise your voice." She sipped her tea calmly.

"Merry, I am a woman-loving woman, I don't want a man nor do I want to play the part of a man!"

"I'm glad, darling."

I was still open-mouthed. "What? You're what?"

She smiled sweetly. "We're going to have sex in a few minutes and I've thought of something different to do."

Dumbly I said, "Different?" I couldn't imagine anything we hadn't done.

Still smiling at me, she put down her cup and pushed back her chair. Undoing buttons, she walked to our bed saying over her shoulder, "Coming, love?"

By the time I got naked she was lying with her legs apart, arms reaching for me.

"Now," she said, "lie on top of me."

I did so and leaned, balancing on my elbows, and looked down at her face, waiting for instructions.

She hooked her legs over my thighs. "Now, darling, move your hips and rub on me."

I did. I moved my hips, feeling her openness beneath me, a nice feeling and, yes, it was sort of different. As sensation spread, I moved more and then more. This stimulation of my body rubbing against hers caused a familiar tension to start building.

Merry began making slight movements, timing them to mine. I rubbed harder, pressing into the raised mound that moved to accommodate me. As I moved, sliding against her, friction caused a heightening of my pleasure. I was in control, I could move faster or harder, whichever felt best. I did both.

There was wetness between us now, my wetness. "Oh Merry, oh Merry," I moaned, my breathing loud in my own ears.

Merry lowered her legs and moved so that I was straddling her thighs. Half sitting, with the warmth of her flesh between my legs, I pressed against her; moving, sliding on the lubricant that flooded from me.

"Merry, oh Merry, I'm coming . . ." I shouted. An instant later, I did, and collapsed onto Merry's softness. She held me tenderly, pulling the cover around us both.

After a moment I said, "If anybody was looking in the door, we'd have looked like a man and a woman having sex. Is that what you were talking about?"

"Yes, darling." She pushed the damp hair back from my forehead. "They call it the missionary position, I believe."

"Well, I may have looked like a man, pumping away on top of you like that but I certainly didn't feel like a man. Were you imagining that I was?"

"No, dearest. You were and always are my own darling. And you are definitely not a man, nor do I ever . . *have* I ever, felt otherwise." Her face in the firelight was serene and full of her love for me.

Satisfied, I said, "Whatever I did, I think I like it."

"You may do it again in a moment, if you wish. But right now I need, very much, to play the missionary myself." And she turned her body onto mine.

Chapter XXII

"Merry, did you mark the calendar?"

"I don't remember if I did or not," Merry answered. "I think I thought you did."

"Nope. Shall I?"

"I guess so. It's so screwed up now that we're probably ten years behind. We should have used a system."

One or the other of us would try to remember to check off each day but we'd forget now and then. When we'd think about it, we'd try to remember how many days had passed. Almost impossible to do. We didn't even know what day of the week it was anymore.

I was studying the calendar. "We should have marked it every time we made love, then we'd remember!"

Merry laughed. "Are you kidding? The darn thing would look like the turkeys danced on it with ink on their feet!"

"That much?"

"You know it!" And she laughed again.

"Well, for your information, today may be November seventh so I have a birthday either tomorrow or yesterday or, maybe, next week."

"You do, darling? I'll have to do something special, won't I?" She turned from the onions and smiled at me.

I nodded, pleased. She turned back to her chopping and I watched her put together the ingredients for our stew. Sometimes my heart filled with so much love that I almost stopped breathing. I treasured each shared moment with this woman to whom I had given my love, my trust, my life.

It did not help to dwell on our circumstances and these days we seldom discussed the why of our being here but I often dreamed of another life with my Merry, one in which we were back in our own time. I saw her happy, laughing, loving me, enjoying our togetherness to the fullest. It saddened me to think too much about what might have been so I busied myself with the water jugs, hauling empty ones out and full ones in.

After supper a couple of days later, Merry made me comfortable on our sofa. "Now," she said, "close your eyes."

I did so, wondering what she could have in mind. We had no presents, no cake, not even paper for birthday wrapping.

"Open your eyes, darling!"

I saw Merry standing before me transformed. She stood provocatively, her arms twined over her head, one hip thrust forward, draped in fired clay beads and bangles which revealed more than they covered. A star was centered on her forehead, tiny beads alternating white and red around her waist and dipping down into that triangle of golden hair. Layers of brown and white beads hung around her neck, from which two lavalieres of yellow stars reached just to her nipples. Brown beads dangled from her ankles. She had remembered the lipstick and her lips were a soft red. Her eyes were accented in white shadow from the ashes of our stove, her lashes long and black. She smiled at me, her teeth white against the red of her lips.

I was very pleased. I knew that she had colored and fired each piece with loving care, using our precious thread to string the decorations together.

"*I* am your birthday present, darling. You now have a dancing girl of your very own to do with as you like. Happy birthday, sweetheart!"

I looked at her, the firelight making shadows dance on the wall behind her as she hummed, as she swayed her hips.

All this time I had seen her with my heart. Now I looked at her with my eyes.

My darling, my one love! The soft, rounded curves that had attracted and held me were gone, melted away. Her breasts, those large delicious mounds of softness that had strained the fabric of whatever she wore, that had caused my heart to pound, were thin now.

Her raised arms revealed rib structure, her hips stood out against the smoothness of her skin. She was thin, almost gaunt. There were scratches on her arms, her hands were red, her nails chipped, dark bruises here and there on her legs and thighs.

I started to cry. The tears began to flow like an open faucet. I couldn't stop. Even with my eyes closed I could see her thinness and I knew that I looked the same. My pants fell down over my hips without the belt to hold them in place. My shirt was much too large, my knees and elbows bony. I bawled helplessly, moaning out loud.

Merry was on her knees. "Chris, darling! Honey, why are you crying?"

I couldn't tell her, I could only sob. She began crying, too, without knowing why I was.

Finally, when I had cried all of the tears in me, I told her, "We are going to die here in this place, just like that child and those people. We're going to starve and waste away to bones . . . if an earthquake doesn't kill us first. Or else we'll work ourselves to death just trying to find food . . . and all that damn wood!"

I found more tears and cried them. "I can't stand seeing you this way, so thin! I love you, Merry, I want you to be safe and warm and have things, not like this . . ."

My voice failed. Finally I got to the stage where I could talk without crying and so we talked about us.

Merry told me that she worried constantly about one of us getting sick or hurt. "Even a toothache would be awful, we would just have to hurt! We don't even have an aspirin." Her hand touched the faint scar on my chin. "I can't stand it when you're hurting!" The thought caused her to sob aloud.

My voice was tight and my head ached from all the crying. "Mostly," I told her, "I think about what you would do if something happened to me and I wasn't here to take care of you. What if you were to fall and break an arm or a leg?" I managed to hold back more tears. "You couldn't take care of yourself, not alone. We don't have clothes warm enough for winter and what we do have is worn out. And what if we run out of wood? Or food? What if we didn't have enough food? And how could we hunt in snow up to our necks? We don't even have gloves!"

The possibilities of horrible things happening were endless. Finally I told her, "Merry, we can't stay here. We have to *do* something!"

She sniffed and wiped both our faces on my ragged shirt. Her eyes were calm now, if very red, and she asked me what I meant.

"There's only one thing, you know it, too. To stay here is to die!"

She nodded, looking into my face.

"So there's only one way I can think of to leave."

She nodded again. "Yes," she said softly, taking my hand in hers, "I know."

* * * * *

So we waited. Except for not gathering wood we did our usual things as the days passed.

The weather did get colder, the skies almost constantly dark with huge clouds on the mountain tops and the snow very near.

Then, this afternoon, I smelled the strange electric odor. It grew stronger as the hours passed.

Now I hear the thunder. It grows louder as it approaches and the lightning is beginning to flash brighter and brighter.

My Merry sits, staring into the fire, her expression calm.

At the first huge crash outside our door, we look at each other. Merry smiles at me, her face is full of love and trust.

I stand, Merry stands. We embrace, then kiss. A soft, tender, loving kiss.

I hear her whisper, "I love you, Chris." But I am too choked to whisper back., I tighten my arms about her slender shoulders and she understands.

I help her with her jacket, then put on my own. Merry picks up Aroma, who rolls her eyes with pleasure.

I take Merry's hand in mine.

"You won't let go?"

I shake my head, no.

We do not close the door.
We walk down the ramp.
To the lightning.

A few of the publications of
THE NAIAD PRESS, INC.
P.O. Box 10543 • Tallahassee, Florida 32302
Phone (904) 539-9322
Mail orders welcome. Please include 15% postage.

TO THE LIGHTNING by Catherine Ennis. 208 pp. Romantic
Lesbian 'Robinson Crusoe' adventure.   ISBN 0-941483-06-1 $8.95

THE OTHER SIDE OF VENUS by Shirley Verel. 224 pp.
Luminous romantic love story.   ISBN 0-941483-07-X   8.95

MEMORY BOARD by Jane Rule. 336 pp. Memorable novel
about an aging Lesbian couple.   ISBN 0-941483-02-9   8.95

THE ALWAYS ANONYMOUS BEAST by Lauren Wright
Douglas. 224 pp. A Caitlin Reese mystery. First in a series.
                ISBN 0-941483-04-5   8.95

SEARCHING FOR SPRING by Patricia A. Murphy. 224 pp.
Novel about the recovery of love.   ISBN 0-941483-00-2   8.95

DUSTY'S QUEEN OF HEARTS DINER by Lee Lynch. 240 pp.
Romantic blue-collar novel.   ISBN 0-941483-01-0   8.95

PARENTS MATTER by Ann Muller. 240 pp. Parents'
relationships with Lesbian daughters and gay sons.
                ISBN 0-930044-91-6   9.95

THE PEARLS by Shelley Smith. 176 pp. Passion and fun in
the Caribbean sun.   ISBN 0-930044-93-2   7.95

MAGDALENA by Sarah Aldridge. 352 pp. Epic Lesbian novel
set on three continents.   ISBN 0-930044-99-1   8.95

THE BLACK AND WHITE OF IT by Ann Allen Shockley.
144 pp. Short stories.   ISBN 0-930044-96-7   7.95

SAY JESUS AND COME TO ME by Ann Allen Shockley. 288
pp. Contemporary romance.   ISBN 0-930044-98-3   8.95

LOVING HER by Ann Allen Shockley. 192 pp. Romantic love
story.   ISBN 0-930044-97-5   7.95

MURDER AT THE NIGHTWOOD BAR by Katherine V.
Forrest. 240 pp. A Kate Delafield mystery. Second in a series.
                ISBN 0-930044-92-4   8.95

ZOE'S BOOK by Gail Pass. 224 pp. Passionate, obsessive love
story.   ISBN 0-930044-95-9   7.95

WINGED DANCER by Camarin Grae. 228 pp. Erotic Lesbian
adventure story.   ISBN 0-930044-88-6   8.95

PAZ by Camarin Grae. 336 pp. Romantic Lesbian adventurer
with the power to change the world.   ISBN 0-930044-89-4   8.95

THIS IS NOT FOR YOU by Jane Rule. 284 pp. A letter to a
beloved is also an intricate novel.   ISBN 0-930044-25-8   7.95

FAULTLINE by Sheila Ortiz Taylor. 140 pp. Warm, funny,
literate story of a startling family.   ISBN 0-930044-24-X   6.95

THE LESBIAN IN LITERATURE by Barbara Grier. 3d ed.
Foreword by Maida Tilchen. 240 pp. Comprehensive bibliography.
Literary ratings; rare photos.   ISBN 0-930044-23-1   7.95

ANNA'S COUNTRY by Elizabeth Lang. 208 pp. A woman
finds her Lesbian identity.   ISBN 0-930044-19-3   6.95

PRISM by Valerie Taylor. 158 pp. A love affair between two
women in their sixties.   ISBN 0-930044-18-5   6.95

BLACK LESBIANS: AN ANNOTATED BIBLIOGRAPHY
compiled by J. R. Roberts. Foreword by Barbara Smith. 112 pp.
Award-winning bibliography.   ISBN 0-930044-21-5   5.95

THE MARQUISE AND THE NOVICE by Victoria Ramstetter.
108 pp. A Lesbian Gothic novel.   ISBN 0-930044-16-9   4.95

OUTLANDER by Jane Rule. 207 pp. Short stories and essays
by one of our finest writers.   ISBN 0-930044-17-7   6.95

SAPPHISTRY: THE BOOK OF LESBIAN SEXUALITY by
Pat Califia. 2d edition, revised. 195 pp.   ISBN 0-9330044-47-9   7.95

ALL TRUE LOVERS by Sarah Aldridge. 292 pp. Romantic
novel set in the 1930s and 1940s.   ISBN 0-930044-10-X   7.95

A WOMAN APPEARED TO ME by Renee Vivien. 65 pp. A
classic; translated by Jeannette H. Foster. ISBN 0-930044-06-1   5.00

CYTHEREA'S BREATH by Sarah Aldridge. 240 pp. Romantic
novel about women's entrance into medicine.
                         ISBN 0-930044-02-9   6.95

TOTTIE by Sarah Aldridge. 181 pp. Lesbian romance in the
turmoil of the sixties.   ISBN 0-930044-01-0   6.95

THE LATECOMER by Sarah Aldridge. 107 pp. A delicate love
story.   ISBN 0-930044-00-2   5.00

ODD GIRL OUT by Ann Bannon.   ISBN 0-930044-83-5   5.95

I AM A WOMAN by Ann Bannon.   ISBN 0-930044-84-3   5.95

WOMEN IN THE SHADOWS by Ann Bannon.
                         ISBN 0-930044-85-1   5.95

JOURNEY TO A WOMAN by Ann Bannon.
                         ISBN 0-930044-86-X   5.95

BEEBO BRINKER by Ann Bannon.   ISBN 0-930044-87-8   5.95
Legendary novels written in the fifties and sixties,
set in the gay mecca of Greenwich Village.

VOLUTE BOOKS

JOURNEY TO FULFILLMENT	Early classics by Valerie	3.95
A WORLD WITHOUT MEN	Taylor: The Erika Frohmann	3.95
RETURN TO LESBOS	series.	3.95

These are just a few of the many Naiad Press titles — we are the oldest and largest lesbian/feminist publishing company in the world. Please request a complete catalog. We offer personal service; we encourage and welcome direct mail orders from individuals who have limited access to bookstores carrying our publications.